Forbidden

ASHLIE SILAS

CHAPTER 1

Katie

I can tell you exactly how it feels to be unable to breathe despite being surrounded by air. Your lungs start to close up, your heart stutters to a stop, and your brain loses the ability to think up rational thoughts.

It's not a panic attack per se. It's more like you're giving up. Like your own body is working against you, your mind wants to shut down. It's like you're drowning. And there aren't any lifeboats, no one to save you.

That's how I feel when I'm underground or in enclosed places or even in elevators.

Like I'm going to die.

PATIENCE IS NOT my strong suit—never has been, never will be. It's especially not my strong suit right now, in this situation. It's 11 p.m., and I'm stuck on the side of the road an hour away from my college campus. The road is deserted and my car won't start.

I dial my best friend's number for the umpteenth time, but

he doesn't pick up. Jameson answered the first time and promised to come get me, but it's been thirty minutes. And now he's ignoring my calls.

It's moments like this that I wonder why I'm even friends with the idiot. But when you've spent the entirety of your life with a person, when you grow up together, there's not really much of a choice. They become a sibling you have to tolerate despite wanting to kill on occasion.

In his defense, Jameson might be on his way already and I should probably stop calling. But I know him, and I know there's a real possibility he's passed out drunk somewhere, having lost his phone and promptly forgotten I exist. Which means I might have to find a way out of this situation myself.

Groaning softly, I step out of the car. The warm crisp air blows onto my face as I do so. For the lack of anything better to do, I glare at my vehicle. The red BMW 428i Gran Coupe was my parents' gift to me when I got into college. I've been driving it for almost four years, and I've been taking really good care of it. I'm not sure what's wrong with it now. I would pop the hood to find out, but judging by the way it stopped and the way the headlights dimmed before the car lost power, I'm pretty sure it's a problem I can't solve tonight.

Which means I've got to find a ride home.

I'm out of luck, though; Friday night means almost eighty percent of the population of NYU is probably at one party or the other. The lesser percentage of people like me who don't go to parties are probably at home, resting in their dorms. Which I should have been doing, until I got it into my head that it would be a nice idea to attend a fashion show. I try calling a cab or an Uber but of course my phone has low signal. It's always right when you need it that the signal bars tend to go on vacation.

Sighing softly, I lean on the car and cross my arms over

my chest. The list of people that I know would drive out to pick me up from campus starts and ends with Jameson. This is the moment that I start to consider my life choices.

I've spent four years at this college and only have one friend. What is wrong with me?

I restart my phone and just when I decide to suck it up and call my older sister for help, headlights start flashing from a distance as a car drives toward me. A few moments ago, I was annoyed that there weren't many cars driving on the road here. That was before I considered the ramifications of being found here by a stranger, all alone.

With gritted teeth, I dial Jameson's number one more time. The call goes to voicemail and I decide to leave him what might be my last words.

"Jamie," I say slowly, "I just want you to know that if I'm kidnapped or killed, I'll come back from the grave and haunt you for ever and ever."

The car finally drives up in front of me. It's a shiny black Mercedes, a new model. Not a car most students at NYU would be driving. A part of me expects the person to keep on going but then they stop right in front of me. The headlights go off and a man steps out of the driver's seat, walking toward me. I back away slowly until I find myself against my car.

My breath catches as I take him in. He's an attractive man and he knows it. It's clear in the way he carries himself, the way he's dressed—a dark blue Armani shirt with its first three buttons undone, crisp black slacks. The man's a personification of messily put together. His dark hair has that just-rolled-out-of-bed look.

When you live in my world, you learn to categorize people based on their appearance, but the man in front of me isn't giving me much to go on.

3

"Hi," he says, stopping in front of me. "Car trouble?"

His voice is husky, sexy with a little lilt that causes unbidden thoughts to run through my head. The man is tan with an exotic look about him that tells me he's probably Cuban, Italian, or Mexican.

"I'm fine," I say, looking away and avoiding his brown eyes. There's something about his deep, piercing gaze that unravels a feeling I can't explain inside of me.

"Really?" he drawls. He looks at my car for a second. "That's a sweet ride. Do you want me to check it out? See if I can fix it? I know my way around cars."

It's nice that he offered, but I shake my head. "There's no need. I think it's the alternator. So unless you've got a new one in your car, there's not much you can do."

His eyes gleam with mild interest. "She knows her way around cars. Interesting."

She also has a taser in her purse. Unfortunately… my purse is in the car.

"What can I do to help?" he asks.

"Nothing. I'm good," I immediately reply.

"So, you want me to just leave you here? On the side of the road in the middle of the night?"

"As opposed to what?" I find myself asking.

"I could give you a ride," he suggests. "I've got a super comfortable car, pretty fast too."

"No thanks."

He tilts his head to the side, those brown eyes peering into mine. "I don't get it. What damsel in distress doesn't want saving?"

My eyes narrow. "I'm not a damsel in distress. My friend's coming to pick me up."

There's no way I'm getting into a car with a stranger.

"Alright," the man agrees. He crosses his arms over his

chest and moves to lean against my car. "Let's wait for this friend together, shall we? Once he gets here, I'll leave."

Warning signals flash in my head. There's no reason a total stranger would want to wait beside me when I'm alone in the middle of the night.

"Actually, I would prefer it if you left. I'll be fine on my own."

He doesn't say anything for several seconds, he just watches me with an amused expression on his face.

"You think I'm a serial killer, don't you? What is it? Is it my devilishly handsome looks? I've heard serial killers tend to be good-looking," he muses.

I have.. no idea what to say to that.

"Don't worry, beautiful. I promise I won't kill you," he says.

"There are far worse things you could do to me than kill me," I mutter.

"I promise I won't do any of the things you've probably conjured in that pretty head of yours."

I sigh. "Could you please go? You're being really nice, but I don't feel comfortable with you here."

He peers at me again, studying me. "You want me to leave?"

"Yes." I nod.

"Like go, go?" he presses.

Does he have hearing problems?

"Yes, I do. Please go."

"Alright, fine," he finally says, pushing off my car. "Since you've refused my aid, I'll leave, princess. Hopefully your Prince Charming gets here quickly. And I really hope you don't run into an actual serial killer."

Would he just go?

"I'm going to leave now," he announces. He doesn't take

5

one step away. "Really, I've got a party to attend on campus and I should get going."

He's obviously stalling, waiting to see if I'll change my mind. It's too bad I'm an incredibly stubborn person.

"Drive safely," I say, waving him off.

He smiles. The smile doesn't feel genuine, but it feels like his. Like the kind of smile he instinctively gives people.

"Careful out here, princess. A lot worse things than me go bump in the night out here."

My eyes find his, and our gazes connect. "Why are you so sure those things are worse than you?"

A smirk this time. "I'm not."

He walks to his car and opens the door. After one last look at me and a small wave, he gets inside, and a few seconds later, he's gone. It isn't until he leaves that I realize that my heart had been racing. It slows down a little with his departure, but now I'm considering the consequences of chasing away someone who had been perfectly willing to help me.

I try to order a cab again but there's none anywhere close to here. This road is practically abandoned this time of the night.

Twenty minutes roll by and now I'm actually regretting chasing away the handsome stranger. Right when I'm gearing up to start walking, headlights flash in the direction the stranger left from. His car rolls to a stop right in front of me and he rolls down his window.

"Hate to break it to you, princess, but I don't think your Prince Charming's coming to save you. Looks like you're stuck with me."

I stare at him in surprise for several seconds. "Didn't you leave?"

"I did. I was about ten minutes away before my

conscience started to kick in. My *mamma* always told me to be a gentleman and help a woman in need. So I stopped and waited for a bit in hopes that your *friend* would show up. He did not," he states.

Embarrassment prickles at my skin. But I'm also kind of touched he went to all that trouble to wait.

"You promise you're not a serial killer, or a rapist, or a terrorist...?"

"You have a pretty wild imagination, don't you?" he asks.

I shrug and he grins.

"I promise to cause you no bodily harm. Or any harm at all."

Satisfied with that, I head to my car and grab my bag, locking it behind me as I walk to the passenger seat of his car. I'll come back for my car in the morning. His scent surrounds me as soon as I enter. Sandalwood mixed with spice mixed with Arabian scents. It's heady and throws me off for a second, I almost forget to breathe.

"Seatbelt, princess," the man rumbles, and the smell-induced haze in my head clears.

I put on the seatbelt and he starts the car. "What's your name?" I ask.

He smiles softly. "Probably a question you should have asked before getting into a car with a stranger."

"You practically forced me in here," I remind him.

He chuckles. "You have a weird way of saying thank you, Princess."

"Katherine," I correct. "My name's Katherine."

"Nice to meet you, Katherine. I'm Topher."

Topher. I say his name over and over in my mind. There's something almost familiar about it, but I can't put my finger on what it is. I decide to let it go.

"So, where am I dropping you off tonight, princess?"

I don't comment on the fact that he's still using the nickname.

"NYU campus, please," I tell him.

He looks to the side for a second before looking back at the road. "You go there?"

"Yeah, last year of college."

"Hmm," he says.

"You?"

"Nah, I'm done with college," he tells me.

He looks young; he can't be that much older than me. Then again, he drives a car that's worth a jillion dollars, so I can't be sure about his age. I can't help but wonder what he does and who his family is. I'm curious, but it wouldn't benefit me to dwell on a man like him.

"Maybe I'll see you around."

My gaze is locked forward as I say, "I doubt it."

Considering I have no plans of ever accepting rides from handsome strangers again.

CHAPTER 2

Topher

G rowing up, my mom would always say to me, "Christopher, why must you make me worried all the time? You need to be careful, *figilia mia.* Learn how to look before you leap."

I've always hated those words. And unfortunately, the only thing my mom's advice ever succeeded in doing was making me want to do the complete opposite. So my philosophy in life is "leap first, look later." Impulsiveness is in my blood. I can't count the number of times I've done incredibly insane shit without thinking it through. But now, as I stand in the opened door of a helicopter, looking down at the expanse of land thousands of miles below, I can't help but think this is one of those moments I should actually consider *mamma's* advice.

I've never been suicidal, but this certainly feels like it's veering into that realm.

Someone claps my back and I turn to glare.

"What's wrong, Toph? Getting cold feet?" Max asks on a laugh.

Maximus Cornelius Terra the Third is a twenty-three-year-old asshole with light blue eyes and shaggy blonde hair. He's just as obnoxious as his name sounds. The guy is set to inherit the Terra empire, and he never lets anyone around him forget it. Sadly, he's also the closest thing I have to a best friend. Although I've never really been in the business of making friends; I just pick up a few stragglers here and there. Max is the one who's stuck around the longest.

"Shut up, man," I mutter, staring down at the ground, which is getting harder and harder to see from up here.

We're being safe. My parachute is already strapped to my back and a safety instructor spent the last thirty minutes teaching us what to do. Still, I can't seem to quiet the racing in my chest. I mentally start counting the people that would shed a tear if I ended up dead. The list is unfortunately short.

My mom would cry, of course. She'd be devastated. My sister-in-law Daniella might shed some tears. My brothers are more likely to shoot someone than cry. The first thing on their minds would be revenge, but there's no revenge to be had when I'm the finisher of my own fate. Ultimately, they'd be disappointed in me.

But that's something I'm used to already. They've been disappointed in me for as long as I can remember.

I take a huge breath and turn to the instructor.

"Hey, gorgeous. Remind me again, how many times have you done this?" I ask over the loud whirring noise of the helicopter.

Her lips pull into a soft smile. "Five times. Each time more exhilarating than the last, Mr. D'Angelo."

"Exhilaration sounds fun," I agree. "Death does not."

"You won't die," she says on a short laugh.

I smirk. "Tell you what, if I make the jump and somehow survive, you'll give me your number?"

Beside me, Max scoffs. I've only got eyes for the instructor, though. She's hot, with perky boobs, long brown hair, and pretty eyes.

"How about you survive first and I'll give you an answer?" she says, batting her eyelashes.

I grin. I might die today, but I'll die knowing I've still got game. Beside me, Max prepares to jump. I get into position, as well.

"Just close your eyes and do it," I say mostly to myself.

Then I notice Max's hand shaking as he holds onto the parachute backpack, and I almost chuckle. He was trying so hard to keep up his bravado while being scared shitless. The cruel part of me wants to push him out, but since I don't want his death on my hands, I motivate him instead.

I take a deep breath and the whir of the helicopter fades away. Everything falls away except myself and this moment. A beat, another breath, and then my body is propelling down to the ground. The wind is in my ears and in that moment, it feels like I can do anything.

The instructor was right. It's absolutely exhilarating.

THE HIGH FROM skydiving follows me throughout the weekend. By the time I show up to work early Monday morning, I'm all smiles, and my employees notice. Ellis and Cara are the only two other mechanics I've hired since I started this business a few months ago.

Toph's Auto Repair Shop.

We only work on sports cars, classic cars, or vintage cars for the elite of New York City. When I proposed the idea to my brother Christian, he had some doubts, but every day, I wake up and show up at work. It feels good to shove it in his face that I'm still sticking to this, despite his earlier misgivings. I'll admit I haven't been the most commendable, consistent person in the world, but working with cars is something I actually love doing, and him helping me build my passion into a career is something I'll always be grateful to my big brothers for. Both of them.

"Hey boss," Cara greets with a little salute.

"What's up, Car?"

"I'm good. You're pretty smiley," she comments, her green eyes studying me.

I shrug. "I had a good weekend. How are things here?"

She moves to stand in front of me, swinging a towel over her shoulder. She's dressed in blue overalls with some engine oil on the side of her face. At first glance, you'd think Cara's a regular tomboy—a girl who likes working with cars and hanging out with guys. But I've also seen her dressed to kill, heading out to clubs on a Friday night. She's great with cars and fucking hot, too. When we first met, most people thought we'd be the ideal match since we're so alike, but Cara's just a friend. We've never left the professional boundaries of what our relationship should entail.

"Pretty great. Someone brought a Cayman in last night," she informs me.

"Sweet," I say, grinning. "What year?"

"2019. Wanna check it out?"

She leads me toward the garage area where all the cars we're currently working on are parked. Ellis is in there working on a Bugatti, but he walks over when he sights us. The three of us pause to marvel at the silver car with red wheels. Cara gives us a breakdown of what the owner wants, then she levels me with a hard stare.

"We need to hire someone else, Toph."

I sigh. She's been pushing for this for the past month.

"I know you're not comfortable with it, but with the three

of us working on the cars, we need someone taking care of the other stuff. Like the financials, client roster, reviews, and all that. We've got a good thing going here and it could be so much bigger. I know it."

Ellis is quiet beside me but I know he agrees with her. He doesn't really talk much. He's got the broody 6'4" man with a big black beard persona down pat. But I trust him. I trust both of them. Ellis helped me out of a bind I found myself in a few years ago, and Cara and I went to school together. She belongs more in the socialite circles in New York than with me, but we get each other. I'm just worried bringing someone new in will affect our dynamic.

"I'll think about it," I tell her, rolling up my sleeves. "Come on, let's get to work."

The three of us disperse, both of them moving to work on their cars while I turn to the beauty in front of me. Cars have always held a special place in my heart, ever since I crashed my dad's Ferrari into a swimming pool when I was sixteen. I almost died that day, but it was totally worth it. Cars speak a language that I'm fluent in. I've always felt more comfortable in the front seat of a sports car than having a conversation with other people.

Before I can slide into the front seat of the Cayman, however, my phone starts ringing. I pull it out of my back pocket and let out a soft breath when I check the caller ID.

"Hey, *fratello*," I greet.

"Topher," Carlo says, his voice low.

My eldest brother seldomly raises his voice. He's a lot more like Christian than me, and sometimes I think even more ruthless, but Carlo never really lets anyone see beneath the surface. He's quiet, and I can't help but wonder if he has any life outside our family. Carlo doesn't seem to care about much else. He shows up. Every damn time. He also judges a lot less than Christian does, so I have that to be grateful for.

"I haven't seen you in two weeks," my brother states.

I chuckle softly. "If you miss me, Lo, just say you miss me."

"Just checking in on you, *fratellino*," he says warmly.

"I'm good," I tell him, leaning against the wall. "At work right now. Someone brought in this sweet Porsche. It's so beautiful, man. The wheels are amazing."

Carlo chuckles. "You never miss an opportunity to gush about cars, do you, Toph?"

"You're the only one always ready to listen," I toss back. "So, what's really going on? Why did you call? Usually, you just text."

"I told you, just checking up on you."

"Bullshit. Chris asked you to, didn't he?"

"Well, we're worried. You haven't been on the front pages of any magazines lately. Christian's worried you're gearing up for some epic fuckup."

Typical Christian.

"And you?"

"I told him you were probably just busy running the shop and that he didn't have to worry about you."

That makes me smile.

"Carlo, you realize I'm Christopher D'Angelo, right? It's always a good idea to be worried about me."

"Alright, so are you going to give me a good reason to be worried anytime soon?" my brother questions.

At that moment, my phone dings with an incoming text. I shift the phone away to read the content and a grin overtakes my face. The text is from Max.

Party at NYU on Friday. Some rich dude's throwing it and it's going to be elite. You'd better not miss this one.

"Actually," I say, still smiling, "there's a very real possibility that I might, *fratello.*"

Carlo sighs. "You know the rules."

"Don't cause a problem so big that not even the D'Angelo name can get me out of it," I state.

"Exactly. While I don't believe there's any such problem," Carlo says, which earns a snort from me, "better safe than sorry. I'll talk to you later, Toph. See you at the next family dinner."

"See you."

He hangs up and I stand still for a few seconds, taking in the dozen cars in the garage. My brothers believe I'm changing, that I'm making a life for myself, building something good. While a part of me would love to prove them right, another part wants so badly not to fit into the box my family wants me to. That's the rebellious side, the side that wants me to be my own man despite not knowing how to do that.

I lean away from the wall to get to work. Before I do, though, something flashes in my mind. A memory of a girl with pretty blue eyes, long blonde hair, and a faulty alternator.

Maybe NYU is exactly where I've got to be come Friday.

CHAPTER 3

Katie

The door slams shut at 7 a.m., just like it does every morning during the week, signaling the departure of my roommate. Francine and I have been living together for two years and I can count on one hand how many times we've sat down to have a conversation.

Her schedule doesn't help, because she's always busy either with school or working one part-time job or the other. I also suspect she doesn't like me much. There's a very real possibility that in her mind, I'm some tasteless rich girl who doesn't do much except spend her daddy's money and wear designer clothing. I'm so much more than that, though. But she's never bothered to get to know me, and I've never been inclined to push it.

Plus, the situation suits me perfectly. Francine is out of the two-bedroom apartment we share first thing in the morning and she doesn't get in until late at night. She spends the weekends at her boyfriend's house, so I basically live here all on my own. Well mostly.

Jameson groans from the floor and I roll my eyes as I sit up, stretching my arms.

"Could you tell your housemate to stop slamming the door like that early in the mornings?" he questions, half-asleep.

I slide down to the floor, delivering an "accidental" kick to the side of his stomach as I head toward my vanity. He groans in pain, curling up on the floor.

"Why would I do that? She's the perfect alarm clock. Thanks to her, I'm up by seven every day," I point out, placing my sleep mask on the table in front of me. I turn to him for a second, observing his position on the floor, "I told you to use the blanket or climb into bed with me."

"Yes, but you were also glaring at me and I got the sense the offer wasn't from the kindness of your heart," my best friend says, getting to his feet. He runs his hand through his brown hair before narrowing his blue eyes in my direction.

"You came in here at one a.m., piss drunk and interrupting my sleep. Did you expect me to be nice?"

"I expected you to guide me into bed slowly and gently. Make sure I was comfortable and also maybe provide a bucket by my side in case I woke up and needed to puke. Instead, you glared at me and called me annoying and a dickhead."

"Do I look like your nanny?"

"You're supposed to take care of me," he whines, lying flat on the bed and pulling my comforter over his head.

I sigh softly. "I'm still pissed at you for Friday."

He lifts the comforter from his head to look at me. "Oh yeah, you still haven't told me about this dude that gave you a ride back to campus. I'm surprised you even got into his car."

"He was... persistent," I admit.

"And good-looking," Jameson says, waggling his eyebrows.

I throw a makeup brush at him. "I never said that!"

"Please, you're blushing at the thought of him. The guy was definitely good-looking, and if he drives a Mercedes, he's definitely rich. How come I haven't seen him around campus?" he muses.

I shrug. "He said he was done with college."

"Done like graduated? Or done like he's a dropout?"

"I don't know. What does it matter?"

"It matters, Katie. We both know it matters. Especially if you're going to have a crush on the guy."

I sputter. "I-I am not crushing on him!"

"Liar," Jameson sings. "Don't worry, I'm not judging. It's time you got some action. And if you were comfortable enough to get into a car with this guy you don't know, then I'm going to guess he's probably a decent person."

"This conversation is irrelevant," I mutter. "I probably won't ever see him again."

Jameson snorts. "Wanna bet?"

THE REST of the week practically flies by. Graduation is in two months and I'm busy with my senior thesis while studying for my final exams. I barely have time for anything other than school. I'm in a café, working on a paper, when I get a call from my dad.

"How's my baby girl?" he asks when I pick up.

I smile as I reply. "I'm good, Daddy. And you? How's work?"

"Fine. There was a counterintelligence case stressing me out a few weeks ago, but we resolved it today. Which is why I thought to call you. We haven't spoken in a while."

"Yeah, but I've been talking to Mom. And I know she tells you everything I say."

He chuckles. "True. It's a good thing your mom's always available to talk to you girls. You know how busy I get."

'I know," I tell him.

"Graduation's in a few months. You haven't told me what your plans are, sweetheart. Would you like me to get you a job? I could get the best one for you. You're still an honors student, right?"

"Yes, Daddy. I am."

I've worked hard to make sure I could make him proud, graduating summa cum laude from college and then moving on to the next step. But these days, I find it hard to visualize what the next step is.

"Actually, I'm not sure I want you to get me a job, Dad. I can find one on my own merit."

He chuckles. "Of course you can. You're my daughter, after all. But you're getting a degree in archaeology, and there are specific places that you're meant to work that might be otherwise hard for you to get to on your own. This is just me giving you a little push."

Meant to work?

A small sigh escapes me. I know my dad well enough that I can read between the lines to understand exactly what he's getting at. He's probably ready to get me a job as the director at a prestigious museum or a consultant at high-class laboratory. Basically, a job he deems worthy of me—but that's not what I want. He's never even asked what I want. And in the past year, what I want has changed pretty greatly.

"I appreciate the push, Dad. But I'll figure out what I want to do on my own."

He sounds a little disappointed, but he doesn't push it. James Malone's biggest talent is knowing which battles to fight and which ones to put off for another day. I'm already dreading the epic fight we're going to have after graduation.

Especially when he finds out I'm not ready to start working in archeology.

I thought it was my dream, and I still love it. I love learning about the past, and about different cultures from around the world. I've never really connected well with my present, and examining the remains of ancient lives has always intrigued me. Which is why I chose to major in anthropology. My dad fought me tooth and nail because he wanted me to choose criminology instead. He wanted to mold me into becoming like him, but ultimately, he let it go.

Now I'm sure he's intent on ensuring I don't do something other than what he chooses, which is pretty hard considering my heart's not in it anymore. I'm sure I'll find my passion again, but after college I don't immediately want to start looking for a job that might end up being my entire life. I just want to be free for a little while. I want to find myself, and I'm not sure how to do it.

My dad keeps me on the phone for a little while longer. He talks to me about everything from the head of the investigations unit that's pissing him off to his worry over my mom's spending habit. I barely say a word, which is okay because he's great at carrying a conversation all on his own. I love my father, but the man's pretty much a narcissist.

"You're still coming over for your mother's birthday dinner, right? I never get to see you anymore, darling."

Because you nitpick over everything and anything when you see me, I think coldly.

"Of course, Dad. I wouldn't miss it for the world."

"Alright. I'll let you get back to what you were doing. Keep making me proud, honey. I love you."

"Love you too, Daddy."

He hangs up and I let out a soft breath. Conversations with my father usually leave me feeling drained. Every day it's a struggle, whether to keep him happy or choose my own happiness. And it's much harder because he truly believes that both things are one and the same. He believes he knows what's best, everyone else be damned.

Jameson suddenly slides into the chair in front of me and I jump a little out of fright. I wasn't expecting to see him.

"What are you doing here?" I ask him.

He's wearing loose-fitting cargos and a black Henley. I raise an eyebrow at the dark shades covering his eyes.

"Are you auditioning for a spy movie or something? Why the shades?" I question. "And how did you find me here?"

"I can always find you," he says. "And the shades are my attempt at being conspicuous on campus. Just in case Abby shows up," he replies.

Abby's his crazy ex. And when I say crazy, I mean batshit insane. She was a sweetheart when their relationship started and by the time they broke up two months later, she was a full-blown stalker. Jameson has always had the worst taste in women. Most of them.

"Just file a restraining order," I tell him, taking a sip of my iced coffee.

He shrugs before leaning forward and swiping one of my cupcakes. I glare, but it barely has any effect. Jameson has been stealing my food since we were five.

"What do you want, anyway? Besides to annoy me."

"You know, one of these days, you'll come to appreciate my amazing presence in your life."

"I doubt that day will come any time soon." I finish my coffee and look at him, giving him my full attention. If he sought me out, it means he wants something, and I want to know what. "Spit it out, Jamie."

He smirks. "You know I love you, right? Like, if they

asked me to name the people I would take a bullet for, the list starts and ends with you."

"You once told me that if Tessa and I were drowning, you'd save her first and leave me to the sharks."

He grins. "I was thirteen and hopelessly in love with your sister. You can't blame me for that."

He says that like he's not still hopelessly in love with her. Jameson has made a move on my older sister more times than I can count. The advances stopped two years ago, however, when Tessa got married.

"I think very differently now," Jameson says.

I raise an eyebrow. "Just tell me what you want."

"Alright, fine." He leans down to whisper conspiratorially. "There's a party tomorrow-"

And that's where I pull the brakes.

"No," I say. "I should have known that's where you were going. Absolutely not, Jameson."

"You didn't even let me finish."

"I'll finish it for you. There's a party tomorrow. You're probably throwing it. I'm guessing it's at your house and you probably need me there to help make sure none of your things get damaged."

His blue eyes widen in surprise. "Damn, Katie. You a mind reader or something?"

"No," I say, getting to my feet. "I just know you, Jameson. And I'm not going to your dumb party."

"Anyone that refers to a party as dumb is uncool, Katherine," he says, getting to his feet as well.

He follows me as I walk out of the café.

"A 21-year-old senior with nothing better to do than spend Friday nights partying and getting drunk is uncool in my book, Jameson."

"What? That's exactly what we should be doing," he states. "Come on, I need you to do me a solid here."

"Get somebody else to do it," I tell him, heading down the path to my house.

It's a twenty-minute walk and I would have brought my car to campus but it's still at the repair shop. Turns out, it wasn't just the alternator that needed fixing. Jameson keeps on following me. We pass by his Range Rover but he doesn't make a move toward it.

"Come on, Katherine. I need you."

Something about the desperation in his voice gives me pause, and I whirl around to face him.

"There's something else. What is it?" I question.

He smirks. "I may have told one of my guys that you'd be there so he would invite this really cool dude to the party."

I blink. "That makes no sense. Explain."

"Fine. You know Maximus, right?"

"Blonde hair, blue eyes, douchey attitude. We went to the same high school, Jamie, of course I know him."

"Well, he's in town, and rumor has it, he's rolling with this really cool guy and any party this guy attends is made infinitely cooler with his presence. We don't need to concern ourselves with the cool guy now," Jameson states. Something flashes in his eyes that makes me suspicious but I don't comment on it. "It's Maximus that has requested your presence. You know he used to have a crush on you, right?"

"No, I don't. And I don't care. I'm not going to a party. I have better things to do with my time than spend a night with a bunch of strangers so drunk they can't see two feet in front of them."

Jameson places his hands on my shoulders, keeping me in place. He leans down to look me in the eye.

"Katie, I want you to listen to me very carefully. We've

known each other since we were in diapers. I know you better than anyone in the entire world. You're my best friend. But honestly, you've really got to let yourself go. I've watched you the past four years. I thought college would finally be a fresh start, an opportunity for you to finally learn how to be free. For once, you would be out from under your dad's thumb. Instead, you chose to do the exact opposite. You folded in on yourself and became even more closed off. I love you, but you can't do that anymore."

My eyes narrow and I shift out of his grip. "Is there a point to this little lecture?"

"I triple dare you," Jameson announces, making me roll my eyes. "You're going to the party tomorrow. You'll have a drink or two, maybe flirt with a guy—it doesn't have to be Maximus. But you're going to have fun. Everyone thinks you're a stuck-up bitch, Katherine. Prove them wrong."

"Maybe I am a stuck-up bitch," I tell him.

"No, you're amazing. And we've only got a few weeks to prove that to everyone else."

'I don't give a fuck about everyone else."

"That's good. But everyone else certainly gives a fuck about you. They're watching you, Katherine. You're a Malone. And they're all curious about what you've got."

I sigh softly. "All this talk just to get me to go to a party."

"It's working, isn't it?" he asks, grinning.

"I'm not going to say no to a triple dare," I mutter.

It's a stupid tradition we made when we were teens. A tradition I have unfortunately been unable to forget.

Jameson lifts me up into a hug. "It'll be amazing. All you've got to do is dress hot, have a few drinks, and enjoy yourself."

"It's going to be a disaster," I say cynically.

24

CHAPTER 4

Topher

I n New York City, the name D'Angelo signifies a crime syndicate. One of the powerful mafia families that rule the underworld in the city. The name inspires fear and, as my brothers like to believe, respect. The motto of our house is "Feared and Respected."

I've always thought it was bullshit. I'm sure we've got the fear down pat, but as for respect, I wouldn't be so sure. Christian likes to believe that one connotes the other. As long as he's feared, he's gaining respect. But real life doesn't work that way. Respect is earned, not forced. And by spreading fear, forcing respect is exactly what my brother is doing.

I don't blame him—as the Don, that's his job. It's all he's ever known. Christian has been training to take over from our father since he was sixteen years old. He might not have been given the title until our dad died, but everyone knew he was meant for it. I was the least likely candidate. Unworthy.

Deep down, I know my father hated it. He hated that I wasn't a made man. He hated that he had been unable to force me into being more like him. Sometimes I imagine making him proud for once, but the only way to do that would probably be by grabbing a gun and shooting a few people.

They all think I'm a coward, but what I'm truly scared of is crossing that line—and being unable to ever find my way back to who I really am. Despite all my misgivings, I own three guns. Because regardless of my philosophy and my belief, I'm still a D'Angelo. And our family name doesn't just earn me respect, it earns me a lot of enemies as well.

My phone starts buzzing as soon as I step outside.

"What?" I ask, picking up the call.

"Are you on your way?" Max questions. I can almost hear the smile in his voice.

"I'm leaving my condo right now. Are you going to tell me the reason you're so excited for tonight? This is the second week in a row you've dragged me to NYU's campus."

"You didn't show up last week, asshole."

"I told you, something came up. I had to give a girl a ride and by the time I dropped her off, I wasn't feeling like partying anymore."

Which was weird. It was the first time in a long time I had actually felt comfortable and at ease with someone. Even when she left, I still couldn't shake off that sense of calm. Katherine barely even talked to me the entire ride to campus, but it was nice regardless. A part of me is hoping I'll run into her tonight. But then again, she doesn't strike me as a party kind of girl.

"Whatever, just get here quick. I need your help charming this girl. For some reason, chicks seem to drift toward you, so if you could please help me out."

That gives me pause. I knew he only wanted me to come for selfish reasons. I could turn around and go back inside; I'm not exactly pumped to play wingman for Max tonight. But staying in on a Friday night just seems sad.

"You can't charm a woman on your own?" I drawl, unlocking my car.

"This girl's special," he mumbles.

Hmm. He actually sounds like he likes her.

"Fine. I'm on my way. Don't hit too much of the happy juice until I get there." If he wants this woman to like him, then he'd better be sober while I work my magic.

Max hangs up and I start the two-hour drive to NYU. With any luck, this guy that's throwing the party has some empty rooms at his house because I'm sure as hell not driving back home tonight.

When I arrive, I stop to wonder who the host actually is. The party's in a luxurious penthouse building a few minutes away from the campus—which tells me whoever this guy is, his parents are probably pretty wealthy. I wonder how much visibility his family has in New York. If they're influential, there's a chance this party could escalate into something that'll be discussed on every blog and in every magazine in the city.

This night might just be interesting.

The party's in full swing by the time I arrive. There are at least a hundred people here and I'm almost positive it will be impossible to find Max in such a dense crowd. But then someone recognizes me and the crowd parts like the sea did for Moses in the bible. To make matters worse, the music stops.

Great.

The whispers start up immediately, and my name travels through the room like wildfire. Thankfully, the D.J has enough sense to start up the music again. Just like that, the party continues, but they know I'm here now. Everyone does.

Max reaches me around the same time two girls appear at my side.

"Hey, you're Topher, right?" the first one asks.

She's wearing a short blue dress that just screams "look at my tits." I respectfully keep my gaze at her eye level. She's pretty, both of them are, but I didn't come to this party to get laid. It suddenly hits me that I'm almost 25 and the thrill of partying, getting wasted, and all that shit is fading.

Damn, Christian's dreams are coming true. I might actually be maturing.

"Yeah," I say slowly. "And you are?"

"I'm Dana. This is my friend, Darla," she introduces.

Dana and Darla, not confusing at all. They start talking to me about how great the party is and how Jameson's so amazing for even throwing it at all. I have no idea who Jameson is. Max finally loses his patience and interrupts Darla mid-rant about how expensive the drinks at clubs are. And how lucky it is that guys like Jameson know how to throw good parties these days. The girls are actually good company.

"Sorry, ladies, but Toph has to help me out with something," Max says, leading me away.

"I'll find you guys," I promise, throwing in a little wink that makes Darla giggle.

Maybe I am in the mood to get laid.

"So, where's your girl?" I ask as he leads me to the pool room, where a couple of guys are playing beer pong. I grit my teeth at the sight. I graduated college three years ago—should I really be here?

"She's not my girl," Max says in frustration. "And I'm pretty sure she's avoiding me. I was talking to her before you arrived and now she's gone."

I clap him on the back. "Ease up, Maximus. It's just a girl."

He glares at me. "Don't call me that."

"Okay, someone's prickly. You need a drink."

One of the guys next to us hears that and points at the keg.

"Aren't you Topher?" he asks, his brown eyes wide and curious.

I swear if I have to hear that question one more time tonight.

"Yeah," I say with a forced smile.

"I heard you chugged down an entire beer keg while hanging upside down at that Hamptons party last year. Dude, you're legendary."

"Thanks, man." At least I know if I die tomorrow, I'll forever be known as the guy who chugged a beer keg upside down. A real mentor for college kids around the world.

"What do you think about showing us your moves? There's a beer keg over there," the kid asks.

Shit. I should have seen that coming.

Unfortunately, the entire room's watching our interaction. I can't simply say no. Plus, Max is too busy sulking in a corner to care. I let out a soft breath and head toward the keg. Chants of my name start up as I get into position and do handstand. When I nod at the keg, someone brings it forward, and I spend the next few minutes of my life chugging cheap beer.

When I'm done, the room erupts in cheers. I want to revel in it, but my gaze is drawn to the doorway of the room. Blue eyes are on me, widened in surprise. It takes me only a second to place her and when I do, a real smile spreads over my face.

Found you.

I hadn't even realized I was looking for her. This was the last place I thought we would meet. Katherine's eyes narrow for a fraction of a second before she smirks and walks away. I manage to maneuver away from the crowd, toward her. She heads for the kitchen area and I follow her in, leaning against the doorway.

"Are you stalking me?" she questions after a few seconds, acknowledging my presence.

There's no one else here but us.

"I was about to ask you the same question. This doesn't seem like your scene, princess."

Her mouth curves slightly but she clears her throat.

"How would you know what my 'scene' is? We barely know each other."

"True, but something tells me you're not a party girl." My eyes latch onto the solo cup in her hands. "I'd bet a hundred dollars there's no alcohol in that cup."

She smiles before lifting the cup to her lips and downing the contents. "I guess we'll never know."

She barely even flinched. It sure as hell wasn't booze.

"What are you doing here?" I ask, pulling myself up and sitting on the kitchen counter. There are several drinks here but I don't pay them any attention.

My eyes are on the woman with ashy blonde hair and intriguing blue eyes. They look like comets. I remember thinking that last week. It's one of the reasons I came back after I left. I couldn't stop thinking about her eyes. There's something about them that just draws a person in.

"It's a party, Topher. I was invited."

I smile at the sound of my name on her lips. Her voice is soft, feminine. "How's your car?"

"You have a lot of questions," she states.

"I'm just curious, princess. This is me catching up on how your week has been since we met."

"Pretty uneventful. This party's the most interesting thing that's happened and I hate it here."

That makes me chuckle. "I knew you weren't a party girl."

She doesn't comment on that. "My car's still at the repair shop. It hasn't gotten fixed yet."

"Hmm," I say. It's on the tip of my tongue to ask her to bring her car to my garage, but Katherine doesn't seem to know anything about me and I'd like to keep the air of mystery for a little while longer.

Her next words surprise me, though.

"Are you a dropout?"

I tilt my head in confusion. "I'm sorry?"

'You said you were done with college. I was wondering if that meant you didn't finish."

"I finished, princess," I say on a laugh. "I didn't go to NYU, but I can assure you I graduated college."

"Where?" she questions.

"I'm not telling. I'm mysterious, you're intrigued. I'd like to keep you intrigued."

"You're not that mysterious," she retorts. "I've always been a pretty good judge of character. I see you, Topher."

"Really?" I drawl. No one ever sees me. "Come on, then. Judge me. What do you think of me?"

Her eyes trail over my face, inquisitive, studying. "You don't like to play by the rules."

I smirk. "I literally just drank a gallon of beer upside down. That's obvious enough."

Her blue eyes narrow in challenge. "Judging by the fact that you're a graduate hanging around a college campus at a party for college students," she emphasizes, "I'm going to say you're immature, probably a rich guy who gets a kick out of being the rebellious son. You lay around all day, spending Daddy's money without a care for anything or anyone."

For the longest moment, I don't say a word. I level her

with a blank stare, not conveying an ounce of emotion at her assessment. She starts to shift under the weight of my gaze, and I can tell she feels a little guilty. She bites the corner of her lip, looking away.

"I'm sorry, that was harsh," she says, blowing out a breath.

"No, it wasn't." I jump down from the kitchen counter. "Nice guess, princess. But you're way off."

I start to walk away but she stops me, placing her hand on my arm.

"Which part? Which part was way off?"

She's curious. "You're trying to figure me out." I smile. "Why?"

"Because you're interesting."

I cross my arms over my chest. "I could say the same thing about you, Katherine."

"So?" she says, insistent on getting an answer to her question.

I consider not replying but decide to at least be honest. "I suppose you were right about some of what you guessed about me. I don't lay around all day, though. I've got a pretty successful business, started it a few months ago, actually. Maybe one day I'll take you to see it."

Her eyes grow a little soft at that. But they widen at my next words.

"As for the part about my 'daddy,' well, I can't very well spend his money if he's dead."

With those words, I walk out of the room, leaving her flustered and shocked.

CHAPTER 5

Katie

Ninety percent of the time, I'm great at saying the right things at the right time. My dad used to tell me I had excellent communication and diplomatic skills. But there are those slim moments, instances where I end up saying the dumbest shit. This is one of those moments.

It takes a few minutes before I go after Topher. When I find him, he's having a conversation with two girls. One blonde, one brunette. His eyes meet mine as I approach.

"Hey," I say, my throat feeling a little hoarse. "I need to talk to you."

Jameson was right. I actually might have a crush on him. And I hate that I might have pushed him away by saying something so stupid. Topher's not the kind of guy I've liked in the past, but something about him pulls me in. He has a magnetic presence, and judging by the way these girls are glaring at me, I'm not the only one feeling it.

"We were talking to him," the blonde states.

Topher moves to stand beside me. "Darla," he says, smiling, "easy there. Katherine and I just have an unresolved conversation to finish. I'll come find you girls later."

Her eyes narrow. "That's what you said the last time. You might be hot stuff but we don't give third chances."

"We can just find someone else," the brunette says. "Bye."

Topher doesn't look the least bit worried. He offers them a small wave and the girls leave. Then he turns to me.

"You just might have cost me an epic threesome, princess."

I make a face at that. "Did I really need to know that?"

"No, but it made you uncomfortable. I like making you uncomfortable," he says, grinning.

"Because it's fun. You like having fun."

"There you go again, trying to fit me into a box. You can't define me. You don't know me at all."

Right. I came here to apologize.

"No, I don't," I agree. "And I'm sorry about what I said. And I'm sorry about your dad."

He waves that off. "It's fine. He died two years ago. I'm over it."

But something in his eyes and the way his body tenses when he says that tells me he's not over it at all.

"I understand complicated family relationships. I love my dad to bits, but on some days, I find myself wishing he didn't exist."

Topher's brown eyes roam my face. "Woah, princess. That's dark."

And it's something I've never admitted out loud to anyone before. I haven't had anything to drink tonight, so I know it's not alcohol making me loose-lipped. It's just Topher and his presence.

"All I'm trying to say is that I get it. Whatever feelings you have about your father and his death are justified."

Topher smiles. "You don't know everything, Katherine. I get the feeling you think you do, but you don't."

"What's that supposed to mean?" I ask, frowning.

"I'll explain better if you get out of here with me," he suggests. "I'm not really feeling the party."

"What about your threesome? If you ask nicely, I'm sure they'd take you back." I grin.

"I'm sure Darla and Dana will find someone else to keep them occupied."

I hesitate. "But—"

"Come on, princess. Leap first, look later," he says. "We both want to get to know each other better. This is our chance. I know a nice restaurant not too far from here we can go to."

Either I'm delusional or he's asking me out on a date.

"You can't drive, you've been drinking."

"You're going to think up every excuse not to go out with me, aren't you?" he questions.

"Maybe," I mutter.

"The beer I chugged was heavily diluted with water, princess. Plus, I have an incredibly high tolerance. Trust me, I'm sober as a judge."

"Sober enough to pass a breathalyzer test?" I argue.

He's amused. "Somebody's a stickler for the rules."

"I'm just worried about us getting pulled over by the cops."

"Okay, fine. I should be able to pass the test if—and that's a pretty big if—we get pulled over. But on the off chance that I don't pass the test, I promise I won't go to jail."

He sounds pretty confident about that, which makes me wonder who he really is. I've been trying to ignore the stares people have been giving him since we walked out of the kitchen. There's more to him than meets the eye.

But he's right. I do want to get to know him.

"Fine, I'll go out with you but I will drive," I say.

"Ok. You have a deal. Your enthusiasm is much appreciated," he says dryly.

I smile. "I just have to find my friend and tell him I'm leaving."

"The same friend who was supposed to come pick you up last week?"

"Good guess," I say under my breath. "I'll meet you outside."

He nods and the crowd of people practically parts for him as he walks out of the room. I search for Jameson, but he finds me first.

"Katie, do my eyes deceive me or did I just see you talking to Christopher D'Angelo?"

And just like that, my blood runs cold.

"Who?"

"Him," Jameson says, pointing in the direction Topher just left. "The third son of the D'Angelo family. I was going to tell you he was coming but I didn't want to freak you out."

"Oh no," I say as it finally dawns on me.

That's why his name sounded so familiar. I've heard it several times when my father has mentioned Topher's family. My heart practically drops.

"I-I need to go," I tell my friend.

"You okay?" Jameson asks worriedly.

"Yeah. I'm just going to go home. I'll tell you everything later, okay?"

"Do you want me to take you home?"

"No, I'm fine. I promise."

Jameson doesn't say anything for several moments. Then

he moves forward to give me a hug. "I'm sorry about tonight, Katie. I never should have forced you out of your comfort zone. And I never should have used you as a bargaining chip to get D'Angelo here."

"Why did you need him here, anyway?" I ask, pulling away from the hug.

"Because his presence means everyone will be talking about this party for a while. He's a D'Angelo, Katie. The wildest of them all."

The wildest of them all—and I was about to go on a date with him. I think I'm going to be sick. Jameson lets me leave after I promise to call him the next morning, and I step outside the building, taking in a shaky breath. My original plan is to head home without having to face him again, but of course, Topher finds me. His brown eyes peer at me, taking note of the expression on my face.

"What's wrong?" he questions.

"You're a D'Angelo." The words sound like an accusation.

It takes a moment for my statement to sink in. And when it does, his expression is immediately guarded, closed off. But not before I catch the way his eyes flash with hurt.

"Is that a problem?" Topher asks slowly.

A laugh bubbles out of me. "You have no idea who I am, do you?"

"Is there something I'm supposed to know?" He sounds really confused.

"My last name is Malone, Topher. Katherine Malone. My dad's the director of the New York FBI office."

That startles a reaction out of him. He blows out a breath.

"Fuck."

Fuck is right. Because I'm pretty sure our families are mortal enemies. I grew up hearing my father rage about the

D'Angelos. Every time he tried to throw one of them in jail, they'd find a way out of it. Murderers and thieves and traffickers. They're not good people, never have been, never will be. And Topher's brother is the head of all of them.

He's probably just like them.

Topher smirks. "You have no idea how open you are, do you, princess? I can practically see your thoughts."

I swallow. "What do you mean?"

"You probably grew up hearing all about my family. Your dad told you stories, scary stories, and now that you know who I am, you're scared. Am I wrong?"

There's nothing kind about his words.

"I just know you're someone I have to stay away from. I knew you were trouble, I just didn't think you'd be dangerous."

He scoffs. "Like I said, Katherine Malone, you don't know shit."

His eyes move above my head and I turn to find Maximus Terra standing behind me. For the love of God, can't he take a hint? Jameson was supposed to keep him away from me tonight, but of course I can't trust him to do anything right. Weirdly enough, Max isn't looking at me. His eyes are on Topher behind me.

"What are you doing with her?"

"This your girl?" Topher questions, his voice low and cold.

"Yeah, why?" Max replies, his expression wary. His eye drift to me for a second.

"You can have her."

Topher leaves immediately after and I'm left wondering what the hell he meant by that. Max walks forward, dropping his arms around my shoulders.

"What did he mean by that?" he drawls.

I push his arm off. "I am not your girl," I say, glaring at him.

Max sighs. "When are you going to stop this game, Katie? It's getting tiring. I want you, you want me. Let's just get together."

"Ew," I say, unable to disguise my disgust. "I don't want you, Max. It's been years, get over yourself."

His jaw clenches and his blue eyes flare. I completely forgot I'm spectacularly good at pissing people off. And now I'm alone outside with a guy who was notorious in high school for being unable to understand that when a girl says no, she means no.

I take a step back.

"Damn, you're a bitch. I was overlooking it because you're smoking hot, but I think it's time you got knocked down a few pegs."

He advances on me and I'm about to scream my lungs out when someone grabs Max from behind. My eyes widen as Topher appears, pushing him to the ground. He tries to get back up, but Topher keeps him down by pressing his shoe against his chest.

"What the fuck!" Max yells.

"I've always been great at choosing questionable company, but I didn't think you were such a shithead that you'd try to hurt a girl."

Max tries to fight his way back up but Topher keeps him down.

"I wasn't going to hurt her," he snaps.

"Liar," Topher says. The fact that he sounds so calm and blasé about the situation is making it even more terrifying. "What were you going to do? Hit her? Maybe force her to kiss you? Would it have made you feel like a man?"

"What the fuck is wrong with you?"

Topher finally releases him from under his feet. Max scrambles up only to be knocked down again by a punch to his face. I gasp, my hand going over my mouth.

"You only get one punch because you didn't touch her. If you had, you'd probably be going home with a broken nose and a few cracked ribs," Topher says calmly.

Max groans, rubbing his jaw.

"Stay the hell away from her, Maximus. I mean it." He turns to me. His eyes soften as soon as they meet mine, and it's almost like nothing happened at all. "I'm taking you home."

What's crazy is that I don't even argue.

By the time we arrive in front of my apartment, I finally find my voice. I unhook my seatbelt, looking at him.

"I appreciate the help tonight," I start. I really do, no one's ever really shown up for me like that when I needed it. No one except my sister. "But I'd appreciate it if you stayed away from me."

He's Christopher D'Angelo. The name spells nothing but trouble, and after what I just witnessed tonight, I'd be lying if I said I wasn't a little bit scared of him.

Topher doesn't even look at me. He nods once before saying, "You've got it."

I take that as a dismissal and step out of the car. I've barely shut the door before he's zooming off.

CHAPTER 6

Topher

TWO MONTHS LATER

My first inclination that my family wasn't normal or treated the same way as everyone else's came when I was eight years old. I convinced my mom to let me go to the playground close to our home for a little bit, and my bodyguard accompanied me. Back then, I hadn't realized it wasn't normal to have a bodyguard follow you everywhere you went.

As soon as we got to the playground, people started whispering and pointing and talking—mostly parents. I could hear snippets of what they said:

"That's the D'Angelo boy."

"Did you hear his father killed that drug kingpin the other day?"

"Such a brutal family. He's a child now, but who knows how he'll turn out when he's older?"

The entire city was talking about us. That day at the playground, parents wouldn't even let their kids near me. And when I told my father, his solution was to threaten the entire neighborhood. After that day, I was only allowed out with the children of other made men in the family. Other kids just like me.

Except they weren't like me, not really. My entire life, I've been sheltered and separated because of my last name. I never used to let it bother me—until I met a beautiful girl whose eyes shone like comets.

The only time I've let myself be hurt in a long time was two months ago. And it's all thanks to Katherine Malone.

"Come on, little man," I prompt. "Just four letters. Say my name."

Daniel's eyes glimmer. They look so much like Christian's. Thankfully, he gets his looks from his mother. My nephew is probably the most precious thing in the world. He's a happy, healthy little boy and the biggest blessing to this family.

I wait patiently to see if he'll say anything or make any noise, but other than a short giggling sound, nothing comes out. I sigh, placing a kiss on his forehead before moving away from the stroller to take a seat at the table.

The rest of my family is already sitting down. Mom's having a conversation with Daniella while Christian and Carlo trade whispered words, tension lining their faces. I'm guessing all's not perfect in the *Cosa Nostra*.

"Done bothering my baby?" Daniella questions when I sit down.

I smile. "How hard is it to say the name 'Toph'?"

"Okay, first off, he hasn't even said 'mama' yet, or 'mom.'"

"Because his first word will be 'dad,'" Christian interjects.

I chuckle at that. Daniella ignores him. "Also, he's six months old. Lay off him, Uncle Toph."

"Shouldn't babies be talking at six months old?" I ask, rubbing my jaw.

My mom offers me a cool look. "You didn't start speaking coherently until you were two, Christopher."

Daniella laughs at that while I roll my eyes. "Nice, *Mamma.* Torment me on my birthday, why don't you?"

"You know I love you, *mia cara,*" she says with a soft smile. "Happy birthday."

"One year older and still a dickhead," Christian says, leaning into his chair.

I flip him off with my middle finger.

"There you go proving my point." He chuckles. "How's the repair shop coming along?"

"Took you long enough," I mutter. "It's coming along fine, Chris. I haven't burned the place down yet. I'll let you know if I do."

"No fighting," Carlo says, trying to keep the peace. "It's Topher's birthday."

"I wouldn't mind it if they fought. What's a D'Angelo birthday without a good old-fashioned brawl?" Daniella says, waggling her eyebrows.

I glare at her. She married into our family a few months ago, and while I used to think that anyone who would willingly do so was crazy, she seems really happy. Happy and in love. Christian's the coldest of us all. The most out of touch with reality, the most inhumane, and yet somehow, he got a woman to fall in love with him.

They have their problems, of course, but now he has a family, a wife and a son. My brother got lucky, and judging by the way he looks at both of them with love and adoration, I can tell he knows it. He deserves it, though. Christian might be an asshole, but I love that he was able to settle down and build a life for himself.

"No fighting!" *Mamma* says authoritatively.

She's 5'3" with short dark hair and eyes exactly like mine. She's tiny, but I've seen her stand up to men much larger than her and put them in their place. It's why her relationship with my dad worked so well. She has always been strong and I admire her so much for it.

"We'll have a nice family lunch, after which we'll play board games to celebrate Topher's birthday."

Christian lets out a chuckle at that. His eyes gleam as he rearranges the cuffs of his black shirt.

"I'm not Topher, Mom, but even I know he wouldn't be caught dead playing board games with us on the night of his birthday."

All eyes swing to me to hear what I have to say to that, and I shrug.

"He's right. Sorry, Mom. I have plans with a couple of my friends tonight."

"He probably means clubbing," Christian says easily.

I glare at him. "You just love getting all up in my shit, don't you?"

"Of course, I do." He smiles. "Have fun tonight, *fratello*."

I'm still glaring when Daniella clears her throat to distract us. "Topher, I haven't seen you entangled with anyone recently. No hook-ups, no girls hanging around you."

"What are you fishing for, *cognata*?" I drawl.

She reaches for a scone in the middle of the table, biting into it with an innocent expression. "Just wondering if you maybe have a girlfriend."

My mother's eyes widen and a grin takes over her face. "You do? Oh, that's wonderful, Christopher. Who's your girlfriend? When will you bring her home?"

Carlo snorts. "He doesn't have a girlfriend."

"Thank you," I grumble. "Where would I even find a girlfriend?"

Daniella frowns. "I was just being hopeful. You've been pretty low-key for a while."

"I've been busy," I tell her, shifting uncomfortably. This family dinner is quickly turning into an inquisition. This is why I don't come over often—everyone's always all up in my business.

"But there are rumors you've been hanging out with—"

"*Tesoro*," Christian says lightly, "he says he doesn't have a girlfriend. Let it go."

Daniella says something under her breath that only he hears, and he smiles softly, taking her hand in his. Just like that, they're stuck in their own little world. Carlo, who's beside me, bumps my shoulder lightly.

"They're just worried about you, *fratello*," he states.

"They worry when I'm causing trouble and they worry when I'm not."

"Exactly," my brother says. "Because you're family."

After lunch, my mom follows me out to my car.

"Be careful, *figilia mia*."

I give her a look. "You know me, *Mamma*. I'm always careful."

The look on her face is serious. "Everyone has a right to be worried, Christopher. You've changed. You smile a lot less these days."

"I'm trying to be better, Mom."

"There was nothing wrong with you before, my sweet boy."

"That wasn't really me, though."

"And this isn't you either. I don't know what happened that caused you to change, but always remember that I love you. Okay? *Per sempre*."

"I love you forever too, *Mamma*."

She gives me a brief hug. "And I really wouldn't mind it if you found a girlfriend. You need the love of a good woman, *mia cara*."

"I doubt I'll find that."

Christian was right when he guessed that my plans for my birthday included a night of clubbing.

"Happy birthday!" several people yell as I walk in.

There are about twenty people in the VIP section of the club when I arrive. Confetti falls onto me, sparkling beneath the dim lighting and tickling my bare skin as it brushes my shoulder. Cara runs up on stilettos and wraps me in a hug.

"Happy birthday, boss. You like?"

I barely know most of these people, but it's the thought that counts. She and I have grown more friendly over the course of the past two months. Mostly because I spent all my time working and she's always there. She's a good friend, and it was sweet of her to throw this party for me.

"It's great. Thanks, Cara," I tell her on a laugh.

I maneuver my way through the people in the room, hugging them and thanking them for the birthday wishes. Soon enough, the focus is off me as more alcohol is brought in and everyone starts dancing and having fun. The party spills onto the main floor of the club, and soon enough, I'm lost at the bottom of endless shot glasses and a heady uninhibited rush in my blood.

Bodies all around me move together, hips rolling, lips touching. I'm currently being rocked by a hot redhead. I'd be lying if I said I wasn't enjoying myself. Running my hands over her neck, I'm about to kiss her when my eyes latch onto something in the corner of the club. Or someone.

Blue eyes. Comets.

My breathing slows and so do my movements. I haven't

46

seen Katherine Malone since she told me to stay away from her. She's noticed me, too. She's standing impossibly still, holding my gaze. Even among hundreds of people, she's all I can concentrate on. The way she glows under the dim lights in the club. The sexy white dress she has on that hugs every curve on her body. She's even more beautiful than I remember.

We continue staring at each other until the spell is broken. A guy approaches her and hands her a drink. Katherine's eyes meet mine once again for a fraction of a second before she throws her head back and downs the shot.

She starts to dance and the guy beside her seems really into it. He seems oddly familiar but I can't even begin to try to place where I know him from. I hate the fact that Katherine's ignoring me and I hate the way her body's moving to the music. She's letting that guy touch her. At first glance, it seems platonic, but when his hand drifts down to the curve of her ass, I snap, pushing forward through the crowd. As soon as I reach them, I grab his hand and shove him off her.

"What the hell!" Katherine yells.

"You should be careful who you dance with at clubs, princess," I say, my eyes not leaving the other guy's green ones.

He seems mildly amused. He crosses his arms over his chest, looking from me to Katherine. The music in changes to something slower and quieter, allowing us to hear each other.

"I was wondering when you'd show up again," the guy says, stretching his hand for a shake. "Hi, I'm Jameson Clyde."

Clyde? Ah, now I remember where I know him from.

"He's my best friend," Katherine says from beside me. "And you're way out of line, Topher."

A muscle ticks in her jaw as she stares up at me.

"You've been drinking," I point out. "I was just making sure you were okay."

"I had one drink. But it doesn't matter because that's none of your business! And I don't need you to make sure I'm okay. We don't know each other."

"He had his hands all over you," I say, staring straight into her eyes. Best friends? The thought almost makes me scoff. They might need to reassess their relationship.

"Jamie gets handsy when he's drunk," she states.

"You always have one defense or the other for him, don't you? He's the one who left you alone that night, isn't he?"

Jameson doesn't even seem mildly offended by that. "You guys talked about me? That's cool."

He reminds me of a golden retriever. I don't think the guy ever lets anything get to him. Actually, he kind of reminds me a little bit of myself. The old me.

"Shut up, Jamie. I'm leaving," Katherine announces. "I was hoping to have one night to myself. But of course, you had to ruin that."

The look in her eyes is one of mild annoyance, coupled with irritation and distrust. She doesn't like me, that much is obvious. And to think all she had to do was find out my last name.

"You're not leaving, Katie," Jameson states. "We're celebrating our graduation. You promised me tonight."

"Promises can be broken," she tells him. "Plus, I danced. I had one drink and now I'm going home. I'll see you tomorrow."

He looks ready to argue but seems to change his mind. Instead, he shifts forward and places a kiss on her forehead. Then he's melting into the crowd, leaving. I turn to Katherine.

"I would say it's nice to see you, but it's not. You look

well. Still partying with reckless abandon?" I can hear the judgment in her voice plain as day.

Resentment builds up inside of me. "Well, congrats on your graduation princess. But it's my birthday so I think I can celebrate also. I have a right to party on my birthday, don't I? Or do D'Angelos not have that right? You going to report me to your dad? Have him throw me in jail?"

Something softens in her eyes. "I didn't know it was your birthday."

"Whatever. You were leaving. So go."

Her eyes flash with hurt. She turns around, walking away. And because I'm a sucker for punishment—or because, for some reason, a part of me is constantly being drawn to her—I follow her out of the club.

CHAPTER 7

Katie

The cold air hits me like a blast as I step outside, but my body heats when I realize there's someone behind me. Of course, he followed me out of the club. I whirl around to face him.

"What do you want?"

He looks great. Two months and he's still just as handsome as I remember. His dark hair is shorter, but other than that, he looks the same. Except he seems sadder. Gone are the easy smiles and I-don't-give-a-fuck attitude I remember. But I could be imagining it.

"You hate me because of my last name," he says, and the words are cold, callous.

"I don't hate you, Topher. I don't know you."

We keep tossing those words back and forth, both of us trying so hard to pretend like we don't know the other when the truth is, he's probably the first person to really see me in a long time.

"Yeah," he agrees, "you don't know me. And yet you don't like me."

I sigh. He's not going to let this go unless I offer an explanation.

"A few years ago, we got a call at home. I was eighteen and the call was from my dad's co-worker. He got shot in the arm during a field operation. A gang war, and he got caught in the middle. Do you want to know who started the gang war?"

Topher smiles without teeth, his eyes dull and shuttered. "My dad always did like exerting dominance over everyone and everything around him."

"Exactly. Your father! Your family's the reason my dad almost died. We could have lost him. I know you weren't there and you probably had nothing to do with it, but I need you to understand that I have no interest in dealing with a guy in the mafia."

A muscle ticks in his jaw. "I'm not in the mafia."

"So you say."

Topher advances toward me, his steps steady. "I'm going to repeat those words slowly so you understand them, princess. I'm not a member of the mafia. My father was and my brothers are, but I am not a part of it."

"What am I supposed to say, congratulations?"

"No. You're supposed to stop looking at me like you're worried I'm going to pull out a weapon and hurt you!"

"You want me to trust that you won't hurt me? You're a D'Angelo, Topher."

"I'm not going to defend the crimes my family has committed. They've done horrible things, I know that. But you also don't get to walk around acting like you're so innocent."

"Compared to you, I'm probably a saint."

He lets those words sink in. Then he sighs and runs his hand through his hair. The earlier tension melts, replaced by a comfort I always feel near him.

"What horrible things are running through your mind? What do you think I've done?"

"Honestly? Probably nothing."

He looks a little relieved by that.

"You think that makes you better than them, don't you?" I ask softly.

His expression is guarded in an instant. "No, I don't."

"Liar," I say, calling him out. "Don't lie to yourself, Topher. You do think you're better than them, but you're not. Just like your brothers, your entire family, the people that work under you, violence is always going to be your gut reaction to everything. You might think you're not like them, but it's in your blood. It's who you are."

He's immediately furious. He moves forward and I take a step back, again and again until my back hits the wall. I let out a soft gasp as my eyes widen.

Topher closes in on me, his scent surrounding me, and despite how dangerous this situation feels and how scared I should be, all I can concentrate on is the fluttering in my chest. And the way he's looking at me right now.

"Stop trying to analyze me. You don't fucking know me," he says through gritted teeth.

"You're angry," I say on a smirk. "Anger means I'm right."

Topher chuckles darkly. "You grow some balls with that shiny new degree you got, princess?"

"I just decided to live freely for the first time."

"And how's that going for you."

"It's... exhilarating."

Something flashes in his brown eyes at that, but he blinks and it's gone. And so is he. He moves away, taking a step back and another.

"You told me to stay away from you."

"I did say that," I agree, refusing to back down.

His eyes study mine like he's searching for something. "I'm going to respect those wishes. Goodbye, princess."

I watch him go, a cold feeling spreading over my chest. "Happy birthday, Topher," I say under my breath.

Whatever is happening between us, however drawn to him I feel, the smart thing to do would be to stay the hell away. Topher might not be as bad as the rest of his family, but that last name is his and that's never going to change.

My life is about to be upended by several changes, and I'm going to stand up to my father for the first time. I'm not letting anything get in the way of that.

———

MY SISTER MASSAGES MY SHOULDERS, prepping me like a boxer about to enter the fighting ring.

"You've got this, Katherine. You're like a panther about to pounce on its prey. All you've got to do is keep your eyes on the target," she says encouragingly at my back.

I laugh. "Chill out, Tess. I'm not going to punch Dad."

She moves from my back to crouch in front of me. Her blue eyes are practically glinting with emotion as she looks at me. If you placed us side by side, it would almost be like seeing double, except Tessa's hair is much darker than mine and she has a beauty mark under her eye that I don't. She's also a few inches taller than me. Aside from that, we're practically twins. But she's the wiser and older one. And the person I look up to the most in the world.

"You're about to make a pretty big decision that goes against what he stands for," Tessa starts. "The only time you've ever done that was when you chose your major. And you only won that fight because I agreed to marry Kyle at the same time so he was less inclined to focus on you. This time, there aren't any distractions. He's going to do his best to change your mind."

"I won't let him," I say softly.

She smiles, running her hand through the ends of my hair. "We both know Dad's as stubborn as a mule."

"Yes, but I've got iron will." Regardless, my sister looks worried. "It'll be okay, Tessa."

We both head to the dining area where Mom and Dad are already seated. My mom looks almost regal seated at his side, beautiful. Her brown eyes are light and playful. All my life, she has always been pretty passive, never really involving herself in our lives. She loves us and has proven that on lots of occasions. But never when it comes to going against Dad. I guess that's why their relationship works so well. Dad would have never survived so long with a strong-willed woman.

Mom smiles at both of us as we take our designated seats. My dad likes a certain order, and since we were young, we've had to follow that order. We had seats assigned to us at the table, times we could use the living room, times to play and times to study. It was constrictive at times, but I grew used to it.

"Tessa," Dad says, focusing on my sister first.

My eyes meet his for a brief moment, blue eyes very much like mine. My sister and I share a lot of our dad's facial features. Mom has complained on several occasions that she did all the work birthing us and yet we look so much like him. At least we have our mother's blonde hair. And Tessa's a lot like her when it comes to mannerisms, always trying to keep the peace.

"You haven't told us why Kyle didn't join us for dinner," Dad points out.

He's growing older, I think. His dark hair's turning gray

and he's not as agile as he used to be. The thought is disconcerting.

"He's busy with work, Daddy," Tessa says lightly.

I observe her for a moment. She hasn't given any inclination that anything is going on, but I know my sister. Something is wrong. But I also know that she wouldn't want me focusing on her problems, not when I've got issues of my own to discuss.

"Is he still having trouble with the board at the company? His family started that company, you'd think they would have more respect."

"Kyle's got it handled, Dad."

He nods and turns to me, but before he can ask the questions I'm sure are swirling in his mind, my mom calls for the staff to bring out our dinner. We eat in silence. There's no noise except for the occasional clacking of our cutlery against the china. As soon as we're done, however, my dad wastes no time in speaking up.

"Katie, you still haven't gotten back to me on the list of places you applied to for work."

I clear my throat. "Yeah, about that, Dad. I haven't applied anywhere."

My dad falls still and my mom's eyes widen. Tessa gives me an encouraging look and a smile.

"Before you freak out, I just want you to know that I'm not trying to deviate from Dad's elaborate plan for my life." Tessa squeezes my leg at that. A clear warning to cut the sass. I carry on. "I just wanted to try something new for a while. Something that doesn't have to do with archaeology."

My father finally finds his voice. "You chose archaeology," he says accusingly. "I wanted you to study criminology. You would have had an amazing career with the F.B.I. You've always been good with people and I was so sure you would have made a great profiler. Instead, you chose to follow your passion. You insisted archaeology was what you wanted to do, and I was content to let you do it."

He fought hard to stop me, but I guess we're going to push that to the side.

"It's still what I want to do, Dad. It's just not what I want to do now."

He leans back in his chair, blue eyes fixed on my face. "So? What do you want to do now? Tell me, Katherine. What's your plan?"

I clear my throat before laying it all out for him. "Graduating top of my class granted me several opportunities. Despite not applying to any companies or museums, I got a couple of decent offers. And those offers will still be there a year or two from now. I spent the past eight years of my life working my ass off and studying. I barely had any time for anything else. I didn't even make any friends. My plan is to build a life for myself, Dad. I don't know who I am, and I want to find myself before I thrust myself into a job that I'll probably be shackled with for the rest of my life."

A muscle ticks in my dad's jaw. "Are you done?"

I nod.

"Good, because I'm only going to say this once. No daughter of mine will remain unemployed while I'm alive. You said you wanted to build a life for yourself, Katherine. I can assure you, the best way to do that is to start now. With a steady job. Making your own money, becoming employed so you can marry well and have a good chance at a future. Instead, you want to do what? Spend your time gallivanting about the city?" He scoffs.

"Dad," I swallow, "you're not hearing me. Nothing's going to change if I start working a little later."

"Everything will change. You'll be behind your peers. It's ridiculous, Katherine. And I'm denying your request."

Tessa tenses beside me. I grit my teeth. This is how it always is with him.

"I'll talk to my friend. He's the director of the Metropolitan Museum of Art. I'm sure you'd like working there, we used to go there all the time when you were little."

I scramble for the right thing to say. He can't just make this decision for me. "Dad, I'm not going to work there."

His eyes narrow. "You're on thin ice, Katie."

"I realize that, and I know you mean well. I understand where your fears are coming from, but I also need you to understand that my feelings are valid, too."

"Your feelings are inconsequential."

The outburst I've been trying to rein in escapes. "You can't force me to get a job if I don't want to!"

The room grows quiet. I don't say a word, and neither does he. My sister and mother are absolutely silent. Tessa would never fight my battles for me, especially ones she can't win. And Mom never fights any battles at all.

"I see," Dad says, his voice reverting to its normal calm. "Alright then, sweetheart. Don't get a job."

Now I'm worried. "What's the catch?"

"Well, it's just hitting me that we might have spoiled you girls too much. Provided you with every luxury you've ever needed. But you're a college graduate now; you've got a degree that you're refusing to put to use. Most people would kill to be in your position, but you don't appreciate it because you already have so much. So I'll take away some of what you have."

Tessa finally speaks. "That sounds ominous, Dad. And scary."

He offers us a half-smile and we wait for him to finish his proclamation.

"There's nothing scary about it. Your sister wants to make adult decisions, so I think it's time for her to be a real adult. Real adults take care of all their bills. And they certainly don't live with their parents."

My jaw drops open. "You're kicking me out?"

"James," Mom mutters uneasily. She gives him a look and they communicate without words for a few seconds. When they're done, Dad turns to me.

"I'm not kicking you out, Katherine. Where would you live? But I am taking away all your credit cards. You'll be expected to take care of your bills and personal expenses from this moment on."

My eyes narrow. "Harsh, Daddy."

"I'm sure you'll be alright. After all, you're trying to 'build a life for yourself.'" He smiles. "Good luck, sweetheart. When you're done trying, let me know. I have the director of the Met on speed dial."

I sigh and lean back in my chair. There's nothing I can do to convince him. This is my punishment and I've got to live with it.

Which means I have to find a job. One that's well-suited for me. Only problem is, I haven't worked a day in my life. I am so freaking screwed.

CHAPTER 8

Topher

Y*ou think you're better than them. But you're not.*
    Katherine's words from two weeks ago have been playing over and over again on a loop in my mind. Do I really think I'm better than my father, than my brothers? They've made some morally questionable decisions. They've killed people and done even worse things. But their motivations were never wrong. They believed they were doing the right thing. They believed they were protecting their families. Do I think I'm better than them because I haven't picked up a gun and shot someone myself?

The truth is, whether I'd like to believe it or not, I've done damage to people not even a gun could have. Just because there was no blood doesn't mean those actions aren't a stain on my soul. So ultimately, no, I'm not better than them. But that's not the problem Katherine pointed out.

The problem is I *think* I am.

With a groan, I roll out from underneath the car I've been working on. Even when I'm trying not to think of her, I end up doing so. It's really starting to piss me off.

Ellis's head pops up and he stares at me from the other

side of our workspace.

"You good, boss?"

I nod once. "Yeah. When's Cara getting back? Lunch breaks are usually thirty minutes," I grumble.

He shrugs. "I wouldn't know, Toph."

When he starts it, the car he's working on gives a soft purr before the engine gutters out. I move closer, eyeing the car worriedly.

"You think it's beyond repair?" I place my hand on my jaw.

Ellis shoots me a grin. "First rule when it comes to cars?"

"Nothing's beyond repair," I reply with a grin of my own. We bump fists and he moves toward the hood of the car while I head for my phone to text Cara.

> Me: You're definitely taking advantage of the fact that I'm your boss.

> Cara: I would never!

I can almost picture her mocking smile.

> Me: Get back here, Car. We've already got so much shit to do.

> Cara: I'm already on my way. Oh, and I'm bringing someone with me.

> Me: Who?

I'm immediately curious. I don't like a lot of people being here. Day in and out, it's just us three and the occasional customer coming to drop or pick up their car.

> Cara: A friend.

That's vague. I arch an eyebrow as I text her back.

> Me: What business does this friend have here?

> Cara: Alright, fine. I took it upon myself to go ahead and find someone suitable for the job. The assistant you should have hired months ago!

My lips pull down to a frown.

> Me: I never asked you to do that.

> Cara: And I did it anyway. Because I'm amazing. Don't get mad, I promise she'll be great at it. I knew her in high school and we recently reconnected. When I met her up with her for lunch, she kept talking about how much she needs a job. Then I remembered she really loves cars and she's, like, hella smart. She could be good for us.

The explanation does nothing to satisfy me. But according to Cara, they're already on their way so I might as well meet this woman.

> Me: Get here quick.

Maybe Cara's right and I'm being ridiculous about not wanting to hire someone else. There's just this part of me that believes that by hiring someone else, I'm making the garage bigger and ruining what I'm already used to. I've got a good thing going here, but one little slip-up and it could all be gone.

Of course, I wake up every day wondering if that slip-up will come from me.

"We're here," Cara announces a few minutes later as she walks through the open garage door.

"Cara," a voice whispers worriedly—a voice I'm all too familiar with. "Why does the sign outside say 'Toph's Auto Repair Shop'?"

Cara turns around to reply, but she doesn't need to. I step forward until I'm face to face with Katherine Malone.

"Because it's mine," I state, staring into her eyes. "Hey there, princess."

This is the moment I have to question if fate has a sick sense of humor. Because why the hell do we keep being thrown together? There's absolutely no reason we should keep meeting like this.

Katherine's startled into silence. She stares wide-eyed at me for several moments before letting out a deep breath.

"Cara, I'm sorry but I have to go," she says, and Cara fixes us both with an appraising look.

"Am I missing something?" she asks.

Katherine gives her a soft smile. "I'll explain later. Thanks for the job offer."

Then, without a backward glance at me, she's exiting the building. My jaw grinds at her hasty retreat but I don't say a word, moving toward the Jeep I had been working on.

"What just happened?" Cara asks, following me.

"Ask your friend," I reply, leaning down to inspect the car's new paint job.

"I'm asking you since you're the one still here."

"Cara, you've got a shitload of work to do. We've all got work to do. And I really don't have time to stand around and talk," I tell her impatiently.

Her eyes narrow, but thankfully, she gets the message and

retreats. A few minutes later, however, Katherine breezes back into the garage, walking up to me.

"What are you doing back here?" I question, staring at her curiously.

"Well, I got outside and then I remembered I came with Cara so I tried to request a ride but couldn't because I don't have a credit card. Or any money for that matter which means, I'm broke and need a job," she mutters.

That startles a laugh out of me. "Excuse me?"

Katherine sighs, moving forward and grabbing my arm. I let her lead me out of the garage until we're standing outside all alone.

"Working with you is a bad idea. But so was pissing my dad off, which led to him cutting me off. I seem to be full of bad ideas these days."

I don't say a word, waiting patiently for her to start making sense.

"I really do know a lot about cars. I've always liked them."

"That's nice, princess."

"And Cara told me you needed someone to help with the things you can't do because you're so busy. Answering phone calls, dealing with clients, sorting through taxes and financials. I can do all that, and I can do it perfectly. I spent a summer in high school working at my dad's office and keeping things afloat. If I can work for James Malone, I can certainly work for you."

"Except," I drawl, latching onto her gaze, "you're forgetting one key factor. I'm not James Malone. I'm Topher D'Angelo. And you hate me."

She opens her mouth to speak. "I don't—"

"Yeah, yeah, I heard you the first time. You don't hate me, you hate my last name. You despise what it's come to stand for and how it's a reminder of what you almost lost. Which is why I'm curious about how you think this little arrangement would ever work."

"Because I'm desperate," she admits, blowing out a breath. Her eyes are warm and tired. "Because I've spent the better part of two weeks trying to find suitable a job and I've failed miserably.

My eyebrow lifts as I cross my arms again. I'd be lying if I said I wasn't enjoying this.

"So I'm all you've got?"

"You're my last option, yes. Either this or a job at Hooters."

"Or you could be a good girl and run back to your daddy."

Her lips set into a hard line. "I'm not going to do that."

"Stubbornness can be one's greatest undoing," I say sagely.

"So can pride," she returns.

"Unfortunately, right now only one of us seems to possess both those attributes in spades."

"Are you going to give me the job or not?" she demands impatiently.

This is a recipe for disaster. And yet I light the fire anyway.

"You can start tomorrow."

She looks relieved, and her blue eyes gleam as she looks at me. I really wish she'd stop looking at me.

"Thank you," she says softly. "And Topher, I'm sorry."

"About?" I prompt. "I can think of a few insults, so you'll have to be more specific princess."

She rolls her eyes. "I'm only sorry about one thing. Judging you because of your last name. Your family might be full of awful people, but that doesn't mean you're an awful person. You're right, I don't know you, and I shouldn't have acted like I did."

I lean closer to whisper in her ear. "Careful, princess. Those awful people you keep mentioning are still my family. And if we're going to work together, you're going to have to learn to keep your biased opinions to yourself, especially when it concerns my family."

She swallows softly and nods. "Friends?"

Her voice is soft, her expression innocent. Seconds tick by as I stare at her stretched hands.

"What are you going to do when your father finds out that you decided to take a job working for a D'Angelo?"

"Let me worry about that," she says fiercely.

When Katherine leaves, Cara's waiting for me as soon as I turn around. She gives me a self-satisfied smirk, her arms crossed over her chest.

"So, how do you know Katie?"

"Right back at you," I murmur, brushing past her and heading inside.

"We went to school together. It's the Upper East Side, Topher. All rich folks know each other."

She's right. My family was pretty isolated growing up, so I'm not exactly immersed in the same social circles as them. Carlo went to a boarding school and then college abroad. Christian was forever a loner, always on the outside looking in. He never really cared about much except the family.

And then there's me. I tried my best to be social, but I never really belonged. When your family's infamous, you're always regarded by everyone warily. It's why despite how pissed I am at the way Katherine's been treating me, I can't blame her. A part of me was just hoping she would be different.

"Katherine's a good person," Cara says suddenly, pulling

me from my thoughts. I turn to look at her with an arched eyebrow. "I'm just saying. I don't know exactly how you know her, or how you two got tangled, but she's a good person. She was kind to me in a school where everyone looked down on me for being the daughter of Corbin Oshiro."

Cara's dad's pretty infamous in our circles, as well. When she was sixteen, he went to jail for embezzlement, tax evasion, and fraud. I can imagine how she must have been treated at school after that happened. I can also imagine Katherine being a decent person and not looking down on her because of her dad's mistakes.

"What's her being a good person got to do with me?" I grumble.

Cara's eyes narrow. "Don't make me regret bringing her here."

"Easy, Car. You're acting like I'll do something terrible to her."

"You might," she shoots back.

"I won't," I say seriously.

Her eyes trail over my face, studying me. "Fine, I believe you. Just remember, Topher. Something terrible includes breaking her heart."

That almost makes me laugh. I doubt I'm capable of doing that. Katherine's not dumb, and I'm pretty sure she's made sure her heart is locked up tight and shielded from me.

"That's not going to happen, Cara. Katherine starts tomorrow. You can show her the ropes when she arrives. And no slacking—you're on thin ice, Oshiro."

She gives me a mock salute before walking away, and I take a second to consider how today has gone. And what Cara said. Katherine working here can only go two ways.

Either nothing happens and I'm worried for nothing—or it ends in an epic disaster.

CHAPTER 9

Katie

My phone buzzes on my pillow beside my face, propelling me out of my dream and right into consciousness. And it's a good thing, too, because my dreams involved light brown eyes and a mischievous smile, and were filled with actions I had no business conjuring up, not even in a subconscious state.

The call's from my sister and I have the good sense to pick it up when it starts to ring again.

"I was making sure you got up early. It's your first day of work, after all and you don't want to be late. And you certainly don't want to piss off your new boss," she chirps in my ear.

I groan, rolling onto my side and clutching my pillow to my chest. I slept late last night because I was busy weighing the pros and cons of working with Topher D'Angelo. The cons made for a pretty extensive list, but the pros won because of one solid point.

I need money.

"I think it's a little too late for that," I tell my sister as I climb off my bed.

"What? What did you do? Please don't tell me you've gotten fired already," Tessa states.

"No! And what do you mean already?"

"Katie, you know I love you to death. But Dad was right when he said you were spoiled. You haven't worked a day in your life and I'm just worried things will go wrong."

"Oh, please," I scoff. "I'll be amazing at my job. I'm Katherine Malone, there's nothing I can't do."

I wish I was actually as confident as those words sounded.

"That's my girl. But what did you mean by it's too late when I mentioned not pissing off your boss?"

"Oh, uh—" I pause and bite my bottom lip. I hate keeping secrets from Tessa, but she feels very strongly about the D'Angelo family. And the mafia in general. My sister's the ultimate goody-two-shoes and there's no way she would support me willingly hanging around a member of the family. "It's nothing, don't worry," I tell her unconvincingly.

"Katherine," she says in a low voice.

"It's fine. Everything's great. I'm going to go to work super early and be the best employee there."

Most importantly, I'm going to prove to Topher that I'm more than just Daddy's little girl.

"You still haven't even told me where you're working," she points out.

"I told you, Cara took me there. It's an auto repair shop. I'll be an assistant, helping out with some administrative and management duties."

"Hmm. Did you do any research to see who owns the shop? You know how dad can get." Tessa presses.

I inwardly groan. "Tess, that's inconsequential. It's not someone you know."

"Fine. As soon as I'm free this week, I'll come check the place out."

That might be a problem. But it's a bridge I'll cross once I get there.

"Dad said you haven't been spending a lot of time at home," my sister adds.

"I've been staying with Jamie."

"And how is he? Jamie?" She tries her best to make her voice flat and unassuming, but there's a slight hitch in her voice that tells me just how much she cares.

My heart aches watching two people I love in such an impossible situation and not being able to do anything about it. I don't think even Tessa's aware of just how much she cares about Jameson. All I know is that the two of them spent one night alone together, trapped in a snowstorm during our vacation to Canada three years ago, and after that, everything changed. The two of them have never talked about it. And I've never asked.

"Jamie's... Jamie," I say on a sigh.

She makes a noise of agreement at that. Like my answer makes perfectly reasonable sense. "I'll let you go. Good luck at work today."

"Thanks, Tess."

She hangs up and I hurriedly get ready before stepping out of my room and into the living room. Jameson is passed out on the couch. I roll my eyes, walking over to poke him in the ribs.

"What is wrong with you, Jamie?" I ask softly.

"I've got a raging headache, Kat. Talk later?" he says, rolling over to continue his sleep. He didn't even open his eyes.

'I'm going to work."

"Alright, I'll see you when you get back," he mumbles sleepily.

I sigh softly, staring at him for a little while longer. He

wasn't always this bad. The drinking and the partying have always been a part of him, but these days, it's like he can't bring himself to care about anything else other than that. He's absent in every way, and I miss my best friend.

I also know the exact moment everything changed. When he changed.

Two years ago, when my sister walked down the aisle and said "I do" to Kyle.

TOPHER PULLS up to work on a motorcycle. I never used to be one of those girls who swooned over bad boys in leather jackets, but as he pulls off the helmet and kills the ignition, my heart skips several beats. He's the embodiment of a man that's bad for you. And yet, I can't help but be a little drawn to him.

Clearing my throat, I choose to focus on something other than the man sauntering toward me.

"Is that a Harley Davidson?" I ask excitedly.

He blinks, looking back at his bike before turning to me. "Yeah... So you really do know a lot about vehicles, huh?"

"My mom once launched a large-scale fashion show that incorporated sports cars and motorcycles. I was twelve, and seeing the models leaning on the vehicles or driving them was pretty damn cool," I tell him.

Topher nods, moving to open the garage door. "Your mom's a designer?"

"Yeah, she has her own fashion brand." It does pretty well despite the fact that she has somewhat put it on a back-burner to take care of us and our family affairs so dad could focus on his career, but with me graduating and dad being at the top of his field, my sister's been helping her out these days. Maybe they can revive it.

"That's nice. How long have you been waiting outside? And why didn't you call?"

"I've been here since eight," I inform him. It's currently 10 a.m. "I did call. I called Cara but she didn't pick up."

Topher smiles as he heads inside the building. "She's not a morning person. She won't get here until around twelve."

"Nice," I mutter. "Way to be an upstanding employer, Toph."

His eyes narrow at the sarcasm. "How about you try to be a little less... stuck up? None of us ever really shows up to work until around ten. We fix cars, no one's coming here for surgery. There don't have to be any rigid rules involved."

I can appreciate the relaxed environment he has but it's certainly not the way I was raised. I believe in structure and enforcing rules that everyone can follow. But Topher has probably lived his entire life breaking rules. I can't expect him to start conforming to them now, let alone make them himself.

"So you were waiting outside for two hours?"

I shrug. "I went to a café not too far from here for a while. Read a little on my tablet."

His eyebrows go up at that. He's standing in front of me now and although we're separated by several feet, he still feels impossibly close.

"Just one question, princess," he starts and I gesture for him to go on. "What did you study in college?"

"I got my degree in archaeology," I reply, wondering where he's going with this.

He looks even more surprised. "So, let me get this straight. You love cars, reading, apparently, and despite all those hobbies, what you studied in college was archaeology. I mean, where did that even come from?"

I assist him in turning on all the lights and he shows me to a desk in the corner of the garage. It's pretty sparse apart from the computer and a landline. I'm guessing this is to be my work space.

I open my mouth to answer him but he stops me.

"Wait, let me guess. You probably used to go to museums a lot and you watched a lot of documentaries involving excavations of past relics when you were little."

My lips curve into a smile. "That's mostly accurate."

"Damn, Katie. You're pretty cool, you know that?"

"Why?" I drawl, leaning against the desk and looking up at him.

He's so much taller than me. It should be intimidating, but it's not. It simply adds to the attraction I refuse to acknowledge. But it does make me wish I liked wearing heels more. Instead, I'm in black sneakers. Which is honestly more practical considering this is an auto-mechanic shop.

"You go after whatever you like. You turn your dreams into reality."

"That's a pretty generous spin on my inability to choose something and stick with it," I say, my voice doing nothing to mask the self-loathing I've felt in the past couple of weeks.

"Bullshit. It's admirable that you can do so much. It's pretty sexy, actually," he says with a wink.

There he is. That's the Topher I met months ago. The one that's constantly trying to charm everyone around him. I almost smile back at him, but I refuse to let him know he has any power over me. I roll my eyes instead.

"My indecisiveness is not sexy. I chose archaeology because of all my probable career paths it was the most passable one. The one my dad wouldn't have fought as hard against."

"What did he want you to do?"

"Become an FBI agent," I reply.

"Hmm. Then I guess it's fortunate you didn't. For the sake of everybody here."

"Why not?"

He leans closer. The movement is so slight, I'm not sure he even realizes it.

"Because then you'd have been trying to get all my secrets," he whispers. "And I have many secrets."

My eyebrows rise in challenge. "How can you be so sure I'm not trying to get all your secrets regardless?"

"That's the intriguing thing about you, Malone. I can't be sure of anything when it comes to you."

With those words, he takes a step back and head toward one of the cars in the garage.

"Get to work, Katie. I already arranged a couple files you need to get through on the laptop. And there's a list of people you need to call to inform them that their cars are fixed, and potential orders we might have to place from other countries."

Topher and I work in silence for the next hour until the third person I saw working here yesterday arrives. I stand up to introduce myself.

"Hi, we didn't get to meet yesterday. I'm Katherine. Or Katie, if you want," I tell him.

"Ellis."

Ellis is an extremely tall man with dark brown complexion, black hair and brown eyes. There's a perpetual frown on his face but he has warm eyes and a calming countenance at the same time.

"Welcome aboard, princess," he tells me, managing a small smile.

Topher chuckles at the nickname and I roll my eyes. Ellis gives me one last smile before he heads over to an area of the garage to change.

"It's just Katie," I call after him.

"Katherine," Topher says on a laugh. "Let it go."

I groan, heading back to my desk. I'm not sure if I like it or hate it here. But I liked speaking with Topher and having a conversation with someone that seems to actually get me.

It doesn't happen often.

CHAPTER 10

Topher

"Question," Katie says, lifting herself onto the hood of my car beside me.

I give her a look because I stepped outside the garage seeking some quality time to think on my own. She smiles and hands me a cup of coffee. I sigh, accepting it and beckoning for her to speak.

"What did you study in college? And what college did you go to?"

I smile. "I really don't want to tell you."

"Why not?"

It's been a few days since she started working here and things have been going well. There haven't been any issues and I'm not sure what I was even worried about in the first place.

Then I look into her eyes and I remember. Too pretty.

"Because my college qualifications might be the only aspect you haven't pegged about me yet. And I like being mysterious," I tell her waggling my eyebrows.

She scoffs. "Please, you're great with cars. Like really, really good from what I can tell. You probably studied mechanical engineering in college or something along that line."

"That's the easy enough part to guess. What do you think, princess? Am I Ivy-League material? Or did I go to a normal college."

Her gaze narrows.

"You probably went to an Ivy-League school," she finally says on a sigh. "With you, it's always good to expect the unexpected. Plus, you seem like exactly the kind of guy that likes to downplay his intelligence."

"I don't downplay anything. I just don't see the need to input my qualifications into every conversation."

"I don't do that," Katie says defensively.

"You do," I tell her with a small smile. "It's fine. It's a product of your upbringing, not necessarily a mirror of your personality."

"Just tell me what college you went to," she grumbles.

"Princeton," I say, to which her eyes widen. "Surprised?"

She shakes her head. "No, like I said. You're exactly the type of guy to downplay how smart he is."

She slides off the car and I follow. "You seem upset," I note.

"I am not."

"It irks you, doesn't it? That I might be smarter than you."

"You *are* smarter than me. And no, it doesn't irk me."

Liar. I don't push it, though. She heads over to her desk and I'm about to follow when someone appears in front of the garage. Carlo walks in like he owns the place and I immediately rush to my brother's side.

"What are you doing here?"

He raises a dark eyebrow. "Visiting my little brother? Why are you so jumpy?"

Fuck, fuck, fuck. The gang war that Katherine's father

was shot in happens to be one of the first times our dad let Christian and Carlo be actively involved in the business. Which means they were probably there, and there's a possibility one of them might have pulled the trigger.

"Nothing. Come on, let's take a walk," I say, placing my hand on his shoulder, intent on getting him out of here.

Carlo wrestles out of my grip, moving toward the rest of my employees.

"Hey, Cara. How's everything going?" he greets.

Cara looks up at him for a fraction of a second. Her cheeks heat, and after a short wave, she goes back to work. My eyes zero in on that encounter.

"Please tell me you didn't," I groan.

"Didn't what?" Carlo asks, a challenge in his eyes.

Never mind, that's a battle I'll fight later. He hasn't noticed Katherine's desk yet and she's intelligently staying away and doing her best to be inconspicuous. I doubt she'd want to meet my brother which is why I need to get him out of here. When my eyes trail over to her, she's seated in front of her laptop, jaw clenched and ignoring everyone and everything. Of course, my looking at her draws Carlo's attention as well.

It only takes him a few seconds and then his expression sours.

"Topher," he says slowly, "why does that woman look so familiar?"

I cross my arms over my chest and stare my brother down. "I don't know what you're talking about."

"Really? Because if I'm remembering correctly, her name's Katherine Malone. Daughter of James Malone. FBI diretor and a man that's sworn on several occasions that he's going to take down our family."

I blow out a breath. One look and he immediately has all

that information. It makes me wonder just how much he knows.

"Her name's not Katherine Malone," I say blandly. "She's Stella Briggs."

Cara lets out a very unhelpful snort and I shoot her an exasperated look.

"Uh-huh," Carlo says. "Come on. Let's take that walk you were talking about."

I follow him out of the building and we start walking down the street. Carlo doesn't say anything for several seconds. When he does speak, his words are in Italian.

"You've been doing so well," he says on a sigh.

That causes me to stiffen.

"I don't know what you're talking about, *fratello*."

"Don't lie to me. At first glance, it seems to me like this is one of your stunts. What are you planning this time? An elaborate scheme that'll cause us a lot of trouble? You going to sell the family's secrets to the FBI?"

I don't even think about it. One minute, I'm trying my best to control my anger, and the next, my hands are on his chest and I'm shoving him back.

"Fuck off, Carlo," I say.

"No! You need to understand that this isn't a game! The family is more than just us, it's Daniella and Daniel and every single capo, every man and woman we take care of. You can't just decide to mess with us on a whim. We're already going through so much shit."

I see the tension lining his body, the anger in his expression. This is about more than just finding Katherine at my garage. Something else is going on.

"What's wrong?"

Carlo doesn't answer.

"I have a right to know," I insist.

"No, you don't. Because you're not one of us. We'll take care of our problems, Christopher. All you need to do is try not to add to them."

My jaw grows tight at his words. "I'm not doing anything to add to them."

"So what are you doing with her?"

"Nothing. We're.." I hesitate. "Friends. Okay? We met a few months ago and I helped her out. Last week, she came here looking for a job and I gave her one because she needed help. There's nothing else going on. This isn't some elaborate scheme. I'm over those."

He looks me in the eye for several seconds. When he's certain I'm telling the truth, he lets out a soft breath.

"Getting involved with Malone's daughter will inevitably get messy, Topher. Regardless of your intentions. The man despises us, and with good reason. Plus, he has a lot of power in New York."

"I know," I tell him.

"Good. Just be careful, okay? I'll try to make sure Christian doesn't find out, but it's only a matter of time before he does. Any chance I could get you to fire her?"

"She hasn't done anything wrong," I grumble. "We haven't done anything wrong."

Other than the heated glances and stares that seem to last moments. But they don't mean anything. I can't let them mean anything.

"Alright. Have it your way, then."

"Are you done railing into me?" I question and he nods once. We start walking back to the garage. "Good. Now when the hell did you get together with Cara?"

Carlo grins. "We ran into each other coincidentally once, and we saw each other casually for a couple of weeks. She broke it off. I never pushed her. The end."

"And you never told me?"

"Why did you need to know?"

"Cara's my employee and she's my friend. You should have told me, Carlo."

He opens his car door and turns back to me. "I'll let you know the next time we decide to have sex."

My lips curl into a smile and I give him a playful shove as he steps into the car. Carlo chuckles softly, turning the ignition.

"Don't forget what I said, Toph. Be careful."

He leaves, and I head straight for Katie's desk.

"What's going through your mind right now, princess?" I question, giving her an appraising look.

Outwardly, she looks pretty calm, which is why I can't tell what she's thinking.

"Nothing," she says gently. "Your brother who is most definitely a murderer just walked into the garage and I'm almost certain he knows who I am. Right now, I'm considering the consequences of staying here. You know just in case they decide to kidnap me in order to force my dad's hand, threaten him or whatever."

Something lodges in my throat at that. "I wouldn't let anyone hurt you."

"You can't protect me from your own family," she says, her eyes bright and fierce.

"My family would never hurt you. We're friends, and trust me, they don't give a fuck about your dad."

I hope. Truthfully, I know nothing about what's going on in the mafia world right now. All I know is that there's some kind of trouble Christian and Carlo are keeping under wraps. It's possible the trouble involves the authorities. But Carlo would have mentioned it if it were like that.

"That's good, I guess, but trust me, my dad certainly gives

a fuck about you and your family."

"They're not going to hurt you, Katherine," I repeat, staring into her eyes to let her know I mean it.

"Okay. I'm going to trust you on that. Because being near you makes me a target, and I don't want to be a target."

"You won't be."

We end up working late into the night. Katherine's trying to straighten out the technicalities involving the shipments of some car parts from Asia. But she keeps hitting a block because it won't get here in time.

She's still on the phone by the time I'm done, trying to convince a customs agent to let the goods enter the country faster. I gesture for her to give me the phone and, after a moment's hesitation, she does. All I need to do is tell the man on the other end my name and he starts stammering out apologies.

"I expect clearance for the shipment in three weeks or less, Mr. Stene," I state.

After an assurance that I'll get the goods, I hand the phone over to Katherine and she ends the call, giving me a weird look.

"It must be pretty nice to just say your name and have doors open up for you. Especially illegal ones."

"Yeah, princess," I say on a laugh. "It's pretty damn awesome."

She frowns, getting to her feet. I wait for her to gather all her stuff and we both head over to her car. The BMW 428i Gran Coupe is a pretty sweet ride, but I'm almost positive it's not going to start tonight. I heard the way it sounded when she drove it in this morning. The car's got some issues that she needs to let me look at. But Katherine's Katherine and she won't let me force her hand into anything. I have to wait for her to realize this stuff on her own.

When she starts the car, smoke billows out from under the hood. She groans, resting her head on the steering wheel, and I grin.

"You're in luck, princess," I tell her. "I've got two helmets."

She doesn't even argue. She steps down from the car and follows me to my motorcycle. There's a gleam in her eyes as she stares at it.

"Go fast," she tells me, grinning.

I chuckle. "Anything you want, princess."

At least she's not one of those chicks that's scared to ride a bike. I straddle the seat and fit the key into the ignition before gesturing for her to climb on. I have to will myself to look away from the bare skin of her thighs as she hops on, tucking her skirt between her legs. She clamps her arms around my waist—not too tightly, but enough that I suck in a soft breath at our closeness.

"Where are we going?"

"Jameson's apartment," she whispers against my back, sounding a little out of breath.

"And why would I take you there and not your home?"

"In what world would I let you within a hundred feet of my house, Topher?" she returns.

Good point.

"Don't you have any other friends I can drop you off with?"

I still remember that "friendly" dance.

Katie sounds amused. "I've been staying at Jameson's house for the past few weeks, Topher. And no, I don't have any other friends to stay with. Either there or nowhere."

I groan softly before starting the engine of the motorcycle. It comes to life with a purr I feel all the way down to my toes. And then we're off.

CHAPTER 11

Katie

"You know you don't have to follow me inside, right?" I ask the infuriating man beside me.

We're standing in front of Jameson's apartment building and I've spent the past two minutes trying to convince Topher to go. My elation from the bike ride is already fading and now I'm just upset he's being a stubborn asshole.

"A gentleman walks a lady to the door after dropping her home," he says in a terrible British accent that makes me want to punch his face.

"Don't be annoying, Topher," I say with a sigh.

"Why don't you want me to come up with you? Is there something you're hiding?"

"Why do you want to come up with me? What could you possibly gain from doing so?" I counter.

He smirks. "I'm curious. I haven't had the chance to get to know Jameson yet and our last encounter wasn't great. Maybe I can see how he's been able to capture your friendship."

"I've known Jameson since we were in diapers," I say. "He's literally the only real friend I've got."

"You're hurting my feelings here, princess."

He's been doing that a lot lately. He keeps referring to us as friends and I haven't corrected him yet. Mostly because I think it's the safest thing we can be. And also because I believe in manifestation. If we say it enough times maybe the things I feel in his presence will magically disappear and I can convince myself not to think of Christopher D'Angelo as anything other than that.

Friends.

"Would you please go?" I plead.

"No," he says, shouldering past me and handing his keys to the valet so his motorcycle is properly parked. I groan, following him into the building. "The last time I was in the apartment, it was filled to the brim with drunk people. I'm just trying to get a feel of how it is when there isn't a raging party."

"It's like a normal house. That I share with my best friend. And if I remember correctly, you were one of those drunk people."

"It was just a little beer," he says, a smile playing on his lips.

I sigh, realizing I have no choice anymore and he was going to walk me up. Topher stays quiet as I walk past the elevators, instead heading for the flight of stairs that lead to the first floor. He doesn't say a word as we start to climb and that more than anything else bothers me.

"Aren't you going to ask?" I say after the third flight of steps.

I look back at him and he's staring at me with an innocent expression.

"Ask what?"

"Why we're using the stairs when there's a perfectly good elevator."

"I thought this was your version of cardio. It's fine, princess. I need the workout as well."

I stop and turn around, staring at him for the longest moment. I can see in his eyes that this is him being nice. For once, he's not going to ask me any uncomfortable questions. Gratitude wells up in my throat but I force it down and turn around, continuing our walk. When we finally arrive in front of the door to the apartment, I grab my key to open it.

As soon as I walk in, a scream is torn from my throat.

Dicks and boobs. Dicks and boobs everywhere.

Topher pulls me behind him as we stare at the shitshow happening in Jameson's living room. He appears a few seconds later, dressed only in a speedo with a grin on his face.

"I didn't think you were coming home, Katie. I thought you'd spend the night at your parents after our conversation last night."

I swallow softly. "If I was going to do that, I would have told you, Jameson. I thought you were joking. Please tell me this isn't what I think it is."

"An orgy," Topher murmurs. He sounds amused.

I'm more shocked.

"D'Angelo, my man," Jameson says excitedly. The two of them fist bump and I roll my eyes. "Since you two are here, you could join the party. The more the merrier."

There's a slight sheen in his eyes that tells me he's not as sober as he appears. He just might be on drugs. My heart clenches. What am I going to do with him?

Topher answers for us. "Actually, Katherine and I are going to leave."

"You sure?"

"Yeah. You have fun. We'll just… yeah."

Jameson doesn't even question it. He simply nods and waves us off. Topher leads me out of the house.

"That was…" he trails off.

"He's not always like that." My voice is a little shaky.

"Eh, he's just having a little fun," Topher says without judgement.

"It's just… the past few years have been hard on him. He lost his mom and then—" I stop before I reveal too much. "He's on a path to self-destruction," I say slowly. "How do you help someone on a path to self-destruction?"

There's a certain desperation in my voice. Topher must see that I'm this close to losing it, because he wraps his arms around my shoulders and rubs them soothingly.

"Hell if I know. Maybe ask my brothers," he says trying to lighten the mood.

Spoken like a man who's probably been in the exact same position.

My eyes well up with tears and I blink them away. "I miss my best friend."

Topher doesn't say a word as I try to pull myself back together. He's like an unshakeable boulder helping me through a hard moment. And when I'm done, he's waiting for me on the other side.

"Jameson's a good person," I say firmly, daring him to contradict that.

"Of course he is, princess. You're a smart girl, I'm sure you'll find a way to help your friend."

We head down the stairs and Topher calls for the valet to bring his motorcycle.

"I'll catch a cab to my parents' house," I tell him.

He arches one eyebrow. "You don't want to go there."

"No. But it's my only other option. I could go to my sister's place, but it's late and I don't want to bother her."

"How about I take you to my house?" He chuckles at whatever expression is on my face. "Relax, Katherine. It's just one night."

"I'm not spending the night with you."

"I'm not asking you to sleep with me. It's a friendly sleep-over at your old pal's place. I'm helping you out of a bind."

"You know, just putting 'friendly' in front of it doesn't change anything."

"What are you talking about?"

His eyes are narrowed in challenge but I'm not going to be the one to comment on whatever this thing is between us. Or the fact that going to his house would be a bad idea. So I shrug.

"Fine, let's go to your place."

I really don't want to have to go home and spend the rest of the night enduring my dad's judgmental expression and his numerous questions.

He gives me a funny look. "Anyone ever tell you that you have a problem with gratitude?"

I smile. "I'll thank you if I survive the night."

I don't add the last part: if I survive the night without doing anything stupid. Like kissing his pretty face.

TOPHER LIVES in a condo that was apparently a gift from his dad before he passed away. It's a pretty nice place. The walls are a gray color, most of the furniture's dark, and there are one or two paintings hanging on the walls. I stare at one for a while.

"You like it?" Topher asks, coming to stand beside me.

"It's pretty. I've never really understood the motivation behind art but I like that it's not straightforward. Art is a reflection of a person's emotions and thoughts. Only the person that creates it has the ability to fully understand what a piece of art is trying to say. Everyone else is just guessing."

"This one was painted by my sister-in-law," Topher states, gesturing at the painting. "She'd love to hear that. I'm pretty sure she'd like you."

"Daniella Evans." It's not a question. I know exactly who his sister-in-law is. Topher raises an eyebrow. "My dad talks about your family a lot."

"And yet," he drawls, "you didn't know who I was when we first met."

"He doesn't talk much about *you*," I clarify with a smile. Why should he? Topher's not a member of the mafia.

"I'll tell Dany what you said. She owns a gallery downtown. You should check it out one day."

A Malone walking into a D'Angelo establishment sounds like the beginning of a disaster.

"Maybe one day," I echo, knowing I probably won't.

Jameson probably would, though. He used to draw a lot before his mom passed away. I don't think he has picked up a pencil since, but I know he loves art. Maybe I could convince him to go to a gallery with me. It might help him.

The thought of Jamie makes me sad and I sigh softly, looking up at Topher.

"I think I need a drink."

He raises an eyebrow. "You don't drink."

"I don't drink often," I correct. "But I indulge on occasion. Come on, it's just a few drinks," I urge him, heading into his kitchen. "I know you've got some good stuff hidden somewhere."

He leans against the doorway as I ransack his kitchen, looking for booze. I finally find a bottle of wine hidden in his cupboard.

"That's expensive," he says slowly.

"Perfect."

"No, not perfect."

He moves forward and grabs the bottle of wine. I pout as he returns it to the cupboard. "We're not drinking that," he says sternly.

I watch as he opens another cupboard, pulling out some whiskey.

"How about this instead?"

I nod in agreement. Then Topher's eyes get that gleam they usually get when he's cooking up something mischievous.

"Care to make this interesting, princess?"

"I'm listening," I say cautiously.

"We can play a game. To get to know each other better. I ask you a question, if you don't want to answer you drink. If you do answer, I drink, and vice versa."

"And the purpose of this game?"

"I told you," he says, grabbing some cups. "Getting to know each other better."

I follow him out of the kitchen and into the living room, settling down on the couch.

"Is there a reason why we can't get to know each other sober?" I ask.

"Why are you single?" He asks.

"Oh, so you're asking personal questions, got it. On second thought, the game sounds great but take it easy."

"Don't worry, I promise not to do anything untoward." His eyes flick over my face, causing my cheeks to heat.

"I would never sleep with you, Topher," I say because, for some reason, I feel the need to clear that up.

"Careful, princess. That almost sounds like a challenge."

"Let's just play your stupid game."

He pours each of us a cup. "I'll go first. Something easy. Body count?"

He watches intently as I pick up the cup and down the contents in one gulp. He doesn't need to know I've only ever slept with two people. Knowing him, he'd probably tease me about it.

Or he could be jealous, a voice whispers in my mind.

I study Topher for a moment. This might be my only chance to figure out how he really feels. About me or even in general. He's so good at hiding things; it would be nice to actually figure him out.

"Have you ever been in love?"

He smiles at the question. "No."

There's no hint of deception in his answer so I roll my eyes and pour myself another drink. By the time we're done playing this game, I'll be wasted.

"How many people have you dated?" Topher questions.

"What is your obsession with the amount of people I've been with?"

He shrugs. "Just indulge me, princess."

"Three. I've dated three guys. Happy?"

There's no visible reaction to my answer.

"Sure." He takes his first drink.

"Who do you love most in the world?" I ask.

"My mom and my nephew. Pretty hard to choose between those two. My brothers and sister-in-law are a close second, though."

I down another drink, ready for his next question. "Who do you love most in the world?"

"My sister. Jameson, my parents," I list.

"Rank them?"

I shake my head. "I can't do that."

"That's fair," Topher says, taking a drink.

"What was your relationship with your dad?"

Topher stiffens. I knew that was the one question that would get to him and I asked it anyway.

He rubs his jaw for a moment before running a hand through his hair. I almost think he's not going to reply.

"My old man and I had a complicated relationship. He loved me, sure, and he was a great father, but ultimately he cared more about my older brothers because they were more like him. I chose not to be like them and that caused a sort of rift between us. I loved him, though. We were a perfectly normal father and son, if we're ignoring the murder and everything else that makes my family who they are. I miss him sometimes, or a lot of the time if I'm being honest. No one ever talks about it, but his death left a really big hole that no one can ever fill. Despite how hard Christian tries."

For several seconds, I have no idea what to say. That was painfully raw. No deceptions or deflections. It's probably the first time Topher's ever opened his heart and let me see him for him. I swallow softly.

"He sounds like a good father," I tell him.

"He was. He wasn't a good man, but he was a great father." Then Topher smiles and I can tell he's done with the subject. "Your turn, princess. Drink so I can ask my next question." I do as he says. "What's the worst thing you've ever done?"

I ponder that question for several seconds before replying vaguely, "I left behind someone I cared about."

I don't explain and he doesn't ask me to. He simply drinks and waits for me to ask my question.

"My turn. Same question," I tell him.

He smiles without teeth. Something crosses his expression, and he doesn't say a word for a long moment. When he does, his confession is surprising. "I slept with a married woman. I didn't know she was married until after the deed had been done. But to be honest, I would've probably slept with her anyways."

I'm not sure how I know that's a lie. But in the brief time I've known him, I've become more attuned to Topher D'Angelo than I realized. Maybe he did do that, but I would bet a thousand bucks that's not the worst thing he has ever done. I don't ask, though, because neither of us has forced the other to answer questions they haven't wanted to all night. I sigh softly and take a drink. Which is when he decides to ask me the next question.

"Why don't you like taking elevators?"

And just like that, all the air is sucked out of my lungs.

"What?" I whisper.

CHAPTER 12

Topher

This was my best attempt at a "I scratch your back, you'll scratch mine" situation, but as soon as I see the look in her eyes, I know without a doubt that Katie's not going to tell me anything. And I have enough sense not to push her. A part of me was hoping telling her about my dad would convince her to talk to me, but it'll clearly take more than that.

"I'll change the question," I tell her, giving her an out. "Have you ever been in love?"

She shakes her head. When she speaks, her voice is soft and light. "Apart from my family and Jameson, no. I don't think I've ever loved anybody."

The more I get to know Katie, the more I realize just how similar we are.

"Your turn to drink, Topher."

I do. The game takes off from there. We stay away from the heavy questions, asking each other light ones instead, like our favorite color, genre of music, things we like to do. It's the most fun I've had with any woman in a platonic sense in forever. Time goes by fast.

Katherine tries to get up to get some water from the kitchen but then she's stumbling and falling into my lap. I hold her in place. "Easy, princess," I chuckle.

"Topher," she says on a giggle, "I think I'm drunk."

"I think so too, sweetheart."

She shifts in my lap, getting comfortable. My breath hitches when her ass bounces against my dick. My jaw grinds as I try to concentrate on not getting hard. But that feels impossible. She's right there in front of me; her scent is in my nostrils, battling against my self-control.

"I'm going to go get you water, Katherine," I tell her, trying to guide her onto the couch.

She keeps me in place, wrapping her arms around my neck. Now we're face to face and I can't help but stare into those mesmerizing blue eyes. Then her gaze flickers to my lips and I know I'm in trouble.

"We're friends, right?" she asks, softly.

"On most days, yeah," I answer gruffly.

She runs her fingertips across the back of my neck. "Can I tell you a secret?"

"Go on."

"I hate being your friend," she whispers in my ear. "I think it's the worst thing ever."

That's the last thing she says before she passes out in my arms. I sigh, lifting her up in my arms and carrying her into my room. I place her on my bed, watching her silently for a few seconds.

"I hate being your friend too, princess," I say softly, placing a kiss on her forehead.

The gentlemanly thing to do would be to step outside and sleep on the couch. But I don't think anyone's ever thought of me as a gentleman. So I strip out of my jeans and shirt before climbing into the opposite side of the bed. I don't expect to fall asleep easily considering how hyperaware I am of Katie's closeness. But that's exactly what lulls me into unconsciousness—the sound of her even breaths and her warmth.

"Holy crap!"

The words are enough to jolt me out of sleep, and my eyes crack open to sunlight flooding my bedroom. Then they move over to the woman beside me on the bed. Katherine's eyes are wide as she stares at me.

"Did you? Did we?" she questions, her eyes filled with accusation.

"Don't worry," I say. "I like my women sober. Trust me, princess, if we fucked, you'd remember it."

A blush tinges her cheeks at that. I slide out of bed and into my closet to pull a shirt over my head. Katherine's eyes track my movements, assessing me quietly.

"You hungry?" I ask her.

She nods and I leave the room, letting her freshen up while I head into the kitchen to prepare us some breakfast. Last night was a roller coaster. I'm not sure just how much she remembers. I'm not sure I even want her to remember. Because her remembering would lead to questions, and I don't think either of us has any answers. At least not now.

Katherine's pleasantly surprised when she steps out of the room to find a spread of toast and eggs and some juice on the table. She gives me a quizzical look.

"You do not seem like the kind of man that can cook."

I shrug. "I'm full of surprises, princess. You, on the other hand, seem like exactly the kind of woman that can't." She scowls. "Go on, prove me wrong."

"There's nothing wrong with being unable to cook," she says, taking a seat at the table.

"There are so many things wrong with it. But I'll lay off you," I state, taking a seat as well. "What do you remember from last night?"

She avoids my eyes, taking a sip of the juice.

"Katherine."

"I don't remember much, okay? I'm drawing a blank from the moment you told me you were in a boy band when you were twelve," she says, grinning.

I smile, too. The boy band was basically my brothers and a few cousins, but our parents dutifully came to watch us, applauding at the end of our show. It's one of my favorite memories.

"So that's all you remember?"

"Yes. Did I do something stupid?" she asks nervously.

I shake my head, relieved. "No."

"Alright. So we're good, right?"

"Sure," I tell her easily. If I'm the only one that remembers, there's no reason to bring it up. "We're good, princess."

Katherine leaves soon after, to go and check on Jameson. I spend the rest of the morning thinking about her and last night.

LATER THAT WEEK, Katherine arrives at work with a huge grin and beelines straight for me. Ever since our sleepover, our dynamic has shifted a little. Before, we were just playacting at being friends, but being with her feels genuine now. While it's not friendship, it's pretty damn close. And Katherine seems intent on pretending it's not more than that.

"Look what I got," she sings, pulling some tickets from an

envelope. "You want to go to a movie premiere? Jameson's dad got him two tickets for his birthday so he could take me, but he's insisting he'd rather spend the night partying."

"So he could take you?" I ask.

"Yeah, why?"

"Why would he assume Jameson would take you?"

"Because I'm his best friend?"

I arch an eyebrow, calling bullshit.

"Alright fine," Katherine sighs. "His dad keeps trying to get us into a relationship."

I roll my eyes.

"We've told him several times that we aren't compatible, but Ricky's a hopeless romantic. He's holding onto hope that his best friend's daughter and his son will have a love story for the ages."

"Huh," I say, moving away to inspect the car I was working on.

"Huh? What does 'huh' mean? Will you go with me or not?"

"Just out of curiosity," I start, "have you and Jameson ever been involved romantically?"

I have to admit that even though there is no way that Katherine and I should be together, I can't help consider the possibilities. We can only play this game for so long but if she's got a thing with her best friend, I need to know now so I can back off. I may be the nicer brother, but I don't want any problems.

Katherine smiles. "You sound jealous, Toph."

"I'm not," I say, although the way my jaw is clenched probably isn't doing much to convince her. "If his dad wants you both together so bad, then why haven't you done it yet?"

"Because we don't have feelings for each other." She says it slowly, like she's explaining it to a child.

"But have you two ever slept together?"

She shakes her head, and I study her expression for a minute. There's something she's not telling me. More to the story than she's letting on. But it's pretty obvious I'm not getting it out of her anytime soon. But she's also telling the truth when she says they don't have any feelings for each other. I pluck one of the tickets from her hand.

"I'll go with you. But we're going to have to take a back door into the theatre. If people see us together, both our families will be on our cases."

"Right."

"Pick you up at eight?"

"I'll meet you there. And it's not a date."

I chuckle. Most days, I like playing along with this little ruse. But sometimes it's fun to rile her up.

"Keep telling yourself that, princess."

We have a great time at the premiere, doing our best to stick to the shadows and appear inconspicuous. Unfortunately, people notice you more exactly when you're trying to not be noticed. Three days later, I get sent a magazine, and in one of the pages, there's a picture of myself and Katie.

We had just finished the movie, and Katie was talking to me about it. I was staring at her intently as she did so. That's the moment the piece of shit photographer decided to capture. We're not doing anything wrong in it, but everyone in New York is going to see the picture. They'll see it and they'll wonder why we're together. James Malone has never made a secret of how much he despises my family.

My jaw clenches and I call Katie, worried about how her father will react to this and if she needs me. But she doesn't answer her phone.

Fuck. I definitely should have seen this coming.

CHAPTER 13

Katie

My sister and I were the perfect kids growing up. We were always so good at doing exactly what our father wanted. Exactly what he told us to do. The one time we didn't do that, it led to a disastrous and traumatic situation. Which is why I've lived most of my life following his wishes.

But at great cost.

When my father returns home from work, he heads straight for my bedroom door. I didn't go to work today and I've been avoiding all calls from Topher. I'm not sure it's a good idea for us to be talking right now.

Three gentle knocks, and I'm rushing to my feet to open the door. My dad's expression is just as I expected it. Calm, gentle. He won't get mad without getting the story straight. My hands are in a fist when he lays down a printed copy of the picture on my bed.

"I had my office ensure that there's nothing wrong with the picture," he starts. "No forgeries, no doctoring, no AI generations. It's legit."

"Of course it's legit, Dad."

He raises an eyebrow. "Really? Because I recognize him. His name's Christopher D'Angelo. Twenty-five years old and the youngest of the three sons of Carmen D'Angelo. Do you know I interrogated him once?"

That makes me rear back in surprise. I shake my head as chills spread through my body.

"A few years ago. He was around twenty at the time and at the center of a big drug operation. His family's supplies, which he stole and used at a party involving minors. He was looking at five, ten years in prison, but his father swooped in and got him out of it. Bribery, blackmail, I'm not sure—the family's pretty resourceful. He might not remember our meeting much, he was pretty out of it when he was brought into custody. The FBI might not have even gotten involved if it wasn't for the large amount of drugs at the party and who his family was."

My dad waits to see my reaction to the story. I don't give him a good one.

"He's not that person anymore, Daddy," I say slowly.

"Oh, really? And since when have you known Christopher well enough to determine what type of person he is?"

"We met a few months ago. When I was still in college," I answer truthfully.

My dad's voice grows sharper. "And you decided to keep it from me?"

"There wasn't anything to tell."

"And now? The two of you seem pretty close in this," he notes, staring at the picture.

"We're friends, Dad. Just friends."

He gets to his feet, pacing the length of my room. I watch him quietly, scared to say something that'll set him off.

"I don't believe I need to remind you about everything that family of criminals has done, Katherine. You know, I made sure you and your sister knew so you would be smart enough to stay the hell away!"

I open my mouth to defend myself but he continues speaking.

"Christopher D'Angelo might not be a made man, but he belongs to a family chock full of them. How could you have forgotten all the horrible things they've done—and still continue to do?"

I swallow softly. "I haven't forgotten. But Topher didn't do anything wrong. He may have been in a bad situation or two but he was just a kid in college dad, trying to be better."

"And now you're defending him."

"He's my friend," I say.

"So you keep saying. Anyway, I'm glad I found out about this 'relationship' before it became something uncontrollable. Listen to me, and listen well, young lady. You'll stay away from Christopher D'Angelo and everything that has to do with the D'Angelo name. Right now, everyone we know is talking about you, probably wondering why you would be around someone like him. You're royalty in these parts, Katherine, and he's practically dirt."

That's funny because Topher's always calling me princess. But I don't think he'd be amused to be compared to dirt. He's the farthest thing from that.

"You can't control everything I do, Dad. Especially not this. Especially when I haven't done anything wrong."

"Are you trying to get yourself killed?" he yells.

We both hear footsteps coming up the steps leading to my room. My mom's face appears in the doorway moments later. She looks from me to Dad worriedly.

"Calm down, James," she murmurs.

I look back at my dad. "Topher and I are friends. This isn't something to freak out over."

He gives my mom an exasperated look. "Are you listening to her? First, she chooses to waste her time by not getting a real job, and now she's consorting with criminals. What is wrong with you, Katherine? What happened to my little girl?"

"I'm still here," I say on a shaky breath.

"No! Because the Katherine I know would have never dared to defy me like this. I'm not sure what this is—a phase, a rebellion—but it ends now. You'll stay right here in this room until you learn to see things my way."

I almost laugh. "I'm not twelve years old, Dad. You can't keep me in here."

His eyes narrow in challenge. "Alright, then I forbid you from seeing the D'Angelo boy. Make the right choice, Katherine. Before you lose your family forever."

He walks out of my room after that declaration. I fall down onto the bed, twirling a snow globe and watching the flakes fall. I turn over what my dad said over and over again. He's right. I have changed. I'm not his little girl anymore. I grew up, and he still can't fathom that I have the ability to make my own decisions. He doesn't trust me at all. He still believes he can order me around like I'm a servant and I'll do his bidding. But I'm capable of dealing with my own problems.

Which is why a few minutes later, I'm getting dressed and leaving the house, finding myself heading to Topher's.

I'm in the mood for self-destruction.

When Topher gets home, he's clearly surprised to find me in front of his front door. Just like always when I'm around him, a tremor starts beneath my skin, buzzing through my body. It's impossible to ignore. I've been fighting it for so long, I'm not sure how to stop.

"You okay?" he asks, his tone wary. "You didn't come into work today."

I don't say a word as he opens the door and asks me inside. Then, from my jacket pocket, I pull out the crumpled picture of us my dad printed. Topher stares at it for a beat before heading toward the kitchen. When he returns, it's with a bottle of water, which he hands to me. I accept it gratefully.

"What did your family say?"

"Carlo already knew we were hanging out so he didn't say anything. Christian was a little pissed. He gave me the usual speech. 'Be careful, this isn't just about you, it's our entire family,' yada, yada, yada. Ultimately, he told me not to do anything stupid. But that's it. His reaction was pretty tame, if I'm being honest. I'm worried something else is going on."

"Oh," I say. "Lucky you."

"What did your dad say?"

"He basically told me I'm a disappointment. And then he forbade me from ever seeing you again."

Topher crosses his arms over his chest. "And yet, here you are... What are you doing here, princess?"

My throat feels a little dry as I speak. "I-I don't know." I get to my feet. "You're right. I shouldn't be here. My dad would kill me if he found out."

Topher fixes me with a cool look but he doesn't make any move to stop me. I don't know what he's waiting for.

"Katherine," he says softly, "why did you come here?"

"Because," I swallow, scared of the next words that will come out of my mouth, "I think I want to have sex with you."

Topher's eyes widen and I feel a rush of satisfaction that I've surprised him.

"I'm going to pretend you didn't say that," he says slowly, unsurely.

"I remember what I said that night," I tell him, "When I got drunk. When I told you I hated being your friend, I meant it. And when I was in your lap, the only thing I could think about was kissing you. I think about it a lot when I'm around you, actually."

Topher's much closer than he was a few minutes ago. Like he's drawn to me. Just like that first night.

"You're doing much better than me, princess," he murmurs. "I think about kissing you all the time."

The intensity in his eyes is like staring directly into a blazing inferno, and I can't take it anymore. I look away and all my bravado falters. What am I doing here? Topher must notice the shift in my countenance before he pushes his hand through my hair, titling my head up so I'm looking at him.

"Don't get scared on me now," he whispers.

"I'm not scared. I'm just wondering if this is a mistake."

"The minute you took a job working for me, you made a mistake, Katie. Now you've got to live with it."

He's right, I know he's right. My scalp tingles where he's holding my hair, and the slight pressure causes my thighs to clench. I rise to my toes so we're much closer. My lips hover close to his, close enough to kiss, close enough to finally put us both out of our misery. My breasts brush against his chest and heat shoots straight to my core.

Pure lust erupts inside me so violently I grow dizzy. I run my hands up his chest; he's hard and warm and he smells so good I could get lost in him. Butterflies dance along my spine. I want nothing more in this moment than to take my clothes off. To drop to my knees and make him feel good. I want his hands on me and I want his head between my legs. My motivations for coming here might have been wrong, but now all I can think about is him.

When I can't take the suspense anymore, I wrap my hand around the back of his neck and drag his lips toward mine.

It's tentative at first, and Topher barely touches me—except his hand that's still in my hair. I think it's a challenge. He wants me to prove how much I want him. I trace his bottom lip with my tongue. I crave his touch more than I've ever craved anything else. I want him so bad.

The tips of my fingers tingle with the need to touch him. They move down to his shirt and lower until they're pressing against the bulge beneath his pants. Topher release a shuddery breath as I trace the outline of his length. He groans and his palm slides down my neck, locking me in place as he finally kisses me like I need him to. My hand is still on his cock and I rub softly, feeling him grow impossibly harder. I frantically undo his belt and zipper.

Our tongues tangle together, stifling my moan as I slip a hand inside his pants. He sucks in a breath when I trace the tip of his cock. I swipe at a bead of arousal with my thumb, rubbing it in circles across his head.

"Fuck," Topher whispers.

His eyes are so dark right now—a telltale sign that he's not in control. He's being driven by desire, lust. His chest rises and falls with each ragged breath. I'm forced to pause in my ministrations when he lifts me into his arms and carries me into his bedroom. He drops me onto the bed and I stare up at him, hoping my expression conveys my need.

He doesn't say a word as I sit up and begin to undress. My dress comes off first and when I unclip my bra, the desire in his eyes intensify. I'm seated on his bed, naked except for my thong. The only sounds in the room are our heavy breathing. Hopefully, he can't hear the pounding of my heart.

"I knew you'd be fucking perfect," he says, still gazing at me in awe.

To spur him into motion, my hand moves to my pussy. I'm so wet and my body craves release. Topher watches as I swirl around the wetness; he watches as I ease one finger inside of me, then another until I'm working myself to the brink.

"I never would have thought you were so passive in the bedroom, Toph," I bait as I continue to finger myself.

A corner of his mouth lifts into a smile. "Don't mind me, beautiful. I'm simply enjoying the view."

"I'd enjoy your hands on me more."

"If I touch you, Katherine, I'm not going to fucking stop."

"Who said anything about stopping?" I moan softly as I tease my clit with my thumb, and that seems to be what breaks him.

He drops to his knees beside the bed and drags me toward the edge—and his face.

Oh my.

I don't think I've ever seen a hotter sight. My entire body buzzes as his tongue darts out, teasing me. I arch my back in response and my thighs squeeze his head between them. He laughs softly, causing my clit to vibrate. My fingers grip onto the sheet as he destroys my ability to form any coherent thoughts. I don't think I've ever been this turned on in my life.

Topher eats pussy like it could be his job. Everything about him is sensual, from the way his nails dig into my thighs to the way he groans softly against me when I moan. The minute he slips a finger inside me, I detonate, coming with a loud cry. My body shudders and my voice is hoarse as I scream his name.

Topher abandons my clit as he sits on top of the bed and pulls me into his arms. He sucks up my cries when his mouth latches onto mine, drawing another shaky breath from me. My lips part and he brushes his tongue against mine, making me taste just how much I want him. When he pulls away to look into my eyes, it steals my breath away.

"I haven't had sex in a while," I find myself confessing.

"Define a while," he drawls.

"Two years," I whisper.

He takes in that information without any outward reaction. Then he kisses my cheek softly. "We don't have to have sex if you don't want to, princess."

"Are you kidding?" I ask, gripping his arms. "I told you that so you would realize just how badly I need you to have sex with me. I'm horny as hell."

That pulls a laugh from him. "You always manage to surprise me, Katherine Malone."

"Is that a yes?"

"To fucking you?" he asks, and I nod. "Hell yes, baby."

He kisses me again and I help him out of his clothes until he's standing in front of me, naked. He called me perfect, but I don't think I could ever hold a candle to him. A part of me can't believe I'm here right now, in this moment, and there's another part that knows deep down this is what I've always wanted.

I kept searching for freedom in the wrong places. Maybe freedom is six feet tall with brown eyes and sinful smiles. Maybe Topher's exactly what I need.

CHAPTER 14

Topher

If someone had told me yesterday that Katherine Malone would be in my bed and begging me to fuck her, I would have called bullshit. She's been in my head for the past few months, but thinking about her always felt more like a fantasy than something I actually worked toward actualizing. Us being together is a disaster of epic proportions. And yet right now, as she lays on my bed naked, I can't think of anything more perfect.

The look on her face as she stares at me is almost enough to quiet the doubts curling in my mind. Because a part of me is worried she's doing this for all the wrong reasons, and I don't want to take advantage of her. Katie doesn't share the same sentiments, though. She runs her hand down my chest, and that simple touch burns like a line of fire.

When her hazy gaze lifts to mine, a ripple of darkness slithers through me. It seems impossible that the lust in her stare is because of me.

"I want this," she breathes, wrapping her fingers around my cock before slowly stroking it from base to head.

A low groan rises up in my throat. "I'm not going to fuck

you slow and sweet. When I fuck, it's rough and hard. You think you can take that, princess?"

There's a challenge in her eyes. "Try me."

In a flash, I have her on her hands and knees. My grip on her hair is tight, but loose enough that she won't feel any pain. I press my hard cock against her ass.

"Has anyone ever taken you here?" I whisper, feeling pressure against my lungs. "Answer me, princess."

Katherine pants. She doesn't resist the hold I have on her hair. "No," she replies.

She glances at me over her shoulder. At the soft look in her eyes, unsure but hot, I lose the ability to think. I run my hands over her ass, molding the soft flesh to fit my palms before slapping it. Katherine inhales sharply and her back arches, her blond hair trailing to her waist. The sight of her on her hands and knees in front of me is so fucking hot. I slap her ass again.

"Ow, Topher," she complains half-heartedly. "Would you just fuck me already?"

I slap her ass, again. Teasing her red thong to the side, I push two fingers inside of her. She clenches down on me so tightly, I groan and pull my fingers free. Katherine lifts one leg up and then the other, allowing me to ease the thong from her body.

When I rub the head of my cock against her pussy, a tremble coasts through her and her fingers grip the sheets.

"We don't have to do this if you're scared," I tell her, even though I'm so far gone that I can barely think.

I need to be inside her more than I need air. Katherine's response is to push her wet heat further against my cock. She's a little tense as I ease inside her, feeding her my cock inch by inch. I caress her ass, saying the most unintelligible shit in an effort to calm her down.

"Fuck, princess. You have no idea how good you feel right now."

I shiver as I slide in further until I'm as deep as I can go. My eyes close for a second; she's gripping me like a tight wet fist. Every cell in my aches for more, but I wait, allowing her to acclimate to my size. After a moment, she rocks back against me, letting me know she's ready. I pull out of her slowly before pushing back in. Katherine groans and drops to her elbows, bracing herself against the headboard.

Her head falls forward and the sight of her biting down on my pillow to quiet her moan sends a rush through my body. I hiss at the pull of her cunt, pressure tightening at the base of my spine. Her ass jiggles with each thrust. She bounces against me, taking me in with lazy strokes. Feeling my control about to explode, I reach forward to rub her clit. The sounds she's making are this close to pushing me over the edge.

"Topher," she cries. "I'm gonna—"

I hold onto her hips with both hands, fucking her through her orgasm. She shudders and clenches around me tightly. My breathing is ragged as I still.

"Will you let me come inside you, baby?" I ask, panting.

She sighs softly. Shit, this is a terrible idea. I hadn't even realized I was fucking her without a condom, but being inside her is the most amazing feeling in the world. Coming inside her would be irresponsible—which is why when I feel the pressure begin to build, I hurriedly pull out and come on her ass instead.

My muscles shake and I fall down onto the bed beside her. Katherine stares at me for a second. I wish I knew what was going on inside her head.

"I'll go get cleaned up," she whispers softly. I nod, unable to even speak right now.

When she returns, she's staring at the bed with an unsure expression on her face.

"Come on," I urge, gesturing for her to come closer.

She climbs in beside me and I pull her head to my chest. When she looks up at me, I can't fight the urge to kiss her softly.

"We'll figure it out in the morning," I tell her as I slowly drift off to sleep.

———

WHEN I WAKE up in the morning, it's to the absence of her heat beside me. By the time I open my eyes, she's getting dressed. Her lips are between her teeth and she looks nervous, scared.

"You were going to leave without saying goodbye?" I ask.

She jumps, hurriedly shielding her bra-clad chest with her dress. I almost roll my eyes, but something tight grips my chest when I realize she isn't looking me in the eye.

"A little too late for that," I say in irritation. "What's wrong with you?"

"Nothing," she mutters, turning around to continue getting dressed.

I don't say a word, leaning against the headboard as I watch her.

"I wasn't thinking straight last night."

She still hasn't looked at me.

"You don't say," I drawl. "Tell me, Katherine. What were you thinking last night? You came to my house and practically threw yourself at me, because…?"

She flinches, either at my words or at my tone.

"I don't know!" she yells, whirling around to face me. "I

was trying to punish my father! And sleeping with you was the worst thing I could think of doing in the moment."

My lips curve into a smirk. I stare at her for several long moments, feeling sick and betrayed all at once.

"You used me," I state.

"No," she says softly as tears well up in her eyes. "It was a mistake. I told you it was a mistake."

"All my life, people have either hated me because of my last name, or they've used me to get what they wanted. Apart from my family, those are the only two types of people I've encountered. And you just became one of them."

Her breath hitches. "I wasn't trying to hurt you."

That makes me chuckle. "You didn't hurt me, princess. It's like you said, I knew it was a mistake and I did it anyway. Unlike you, I didn't do it to piss off my father, I did it because I wanted to. Because I wanted to prove to myself that I could."

I see the moment she realizes what I'm trying to say. My words are cruel and biting and absolute lies—and they have the desired effect.

"You're saying sleeping with me was some sort of conquest," she says dully.

"I'm saying ultimately, we both used each other. Leave, Katherine. I would show you to the door, but I'm a little indecent."

She's hurt; I can tell she's hurt but she's trying to pretend she's not. She stares me down, standing tall despite the way her hands shake.

"I'll see myself out."

My jaw is clenched as she walks out without a backward glance. My hand twitches and I curl it into a fist, resisting the urge to go after her and tell her I was wrong.

Because I wasn't fucking wrong. She used me, and I

wasn't about to let her go on thinking her actions hurt me or had any effect on me whatsoever. Something cold settles and presses against my chest as I grit my teeth.

I knew. I knew from the start getting involved with Katherine Malone was a mistake. And I did it anyway because I couldn't stay away.

We both made mistakes. And now we've got to live with them.

———

MY KEYS jangle from my hand as I head into my mother's apartment building. She summoned me a few days ago and I can't avoid her anymore. She threatened to literally barge into my place of work and drag me by the ear to her car. And knowing my *mamma*, she wasn't playing about that. I raise a hand to greet the capo that's been assigned to her protection detail. He's usually around the building to make sure she doesn't run into any danger. Mom hates his presence, but she hasn't got any choice. The wife of a former Don is just as vulnerable even after his death.

The elevator ride takes only two minutes, and in those two minutes, my mind flashes to the image of Katherine's face when I asked her why she doesn't like elevators. She was scared, frightened even, which means there's more to it than I'll probably ever know. I'll always be curious, though.

She keeps up such a strong front all the time. What could make a woman like her scared?

By the time I arrive at my mother's door, the easy expression on my face and my light mood have vanished. Thoughts of Katherine have altered my mood entirely. technically, I'm not angry at Katherine. When I think about how things went down between us, all I feel is this ache in my chest. We slept together for the wrong reasons.

It wouldn't be the first time I've done that, and I doubt it'll be the last. The situation with Katherine doesn't have to be special. When my mom opens the door, however, I force a smile, leaning down to kiss her forehead.

"There's my favorite lady," I say, brushing past her into the house. I raise an eyebrow at her appearance. "What are you up to, *mamma*?"

She pats down on the front of her apron, cleaning off puffs of something white. I'm guessing it's flour. There's some on her face, as well. She lets out an irritated sigh as she heads into the kitchen and I follow. There are several cracked eggs on the counter, sugar everywhere, and basically, it's a disaster.

I arch an eyebrow with a smile.

"Oh, shut it, Topher. Baking's not as easy as I thought it would be," she mutters, leaning against the counter and crossing her arms.

I chuckle. "What even brought this on? You've never wanted to spend any time in the kitchen before."

My mom's an oddity of an Italian woman. She's terrible at cooking, or any kind of manual labor, really. My brothers and I spent the majority of our childhood being fed by a chef my father hired.

"Yes, but I was with Dany and Daniel a few days ago and she was cooking in the kitchen and he was watching her with such an adorable expression on his face. And I wanted to be able to spend time with him like that," she says sadly.

My eyes latch onto the expression on her face and something inside me splinters. I hate seeing my mom sad. She's the most important person in the world to me. With a sigh, I step forward and pull my arms around her. She rests her head on my chest.

"I'm sure Daniel will want to spend time with you even if you can't cook, *Mamma*. Honestly, I don't think he has much of a choice, considering he's a baby," I say on a laugh.

"I'm just worried. I don't want to be irrelevant in their lives. In all of your lives. You boys don't come to see me that much anymore and I feel so useless."

Guilt hits me squarely in the chest. I clear my throat and look away from my mom for a second, trying to gather my thoughts. I hadn't realized she was feeling that way. But I can't be too surprised. Since Dad died, she's been drifting. He was her anchor and now that he's not here anymore, I can't imagine it's easy.

"We're assholes."

Her eyes narrow at that and I quickly correct myself.

"Sorry. I'm just saying that we were wrong to ever let you feel like that."

She smiles. "It's alright, *mia cara*. You couldn't have known. Just ignore the feelings of an old woman with nothing to do with her time."

She moves away and I run my hand through my hair as I try to think of a solution.

"You could get a hobby. One that doesn't involve cooking," I say pointedly.

She laughs. "What hobby would I get, *cara*? I hadn't realized how much of my life revolved around your father until he was gone."

"You miss him a lot."

"Your father was my bright light," she agrees with a nod.

"Mom, how do you…?" I pause, unsure how she'll take the question. But the expression on her face is patient and encouraging. "How did you fall in love with someone like him?"

"You're asking how I could ignore the fact that your father was a ruthless murderer, and all his other faults?"

I nod, and she smiles.

"Christopher, your father wasn't a good man, I'm sure you know that. He wasn't moral and neither are your brothers. I didn't ignore his faults, *mia cara*. I just learned to accept them."

"You accepted his darkness," I say dully. "You made yourself complicit in all his crimes. You fell in love with someone a lot of people considered to be a monster."

"He wasn't a monster to me, my love. He was amazing. He loved me, he protected me. He was the first person that let me be who I was. I truly found myself when I was with your father. I don't ever want you to think of him as a monster, Topher. Because he did it all for us. He's the reason you're standing here today, strong and happy."

My mind flashes to Katherine at my mom's words. Mom found herself when she was with Dad. I have an inkling of how that feels. For a few hours, Katherine was mine. She was in my arms and I was happy. I hadn't realized how much of a void I had in me until she filled it momentarily. And now she's gone. And I don't know how to get her back. I don't even know if I should.

"I'm not... I'm not really happy, *Mamma*. I haven't been happy in a long time."

It's ironic. Of all my brothers, I was the only one allowed to keep parts of my soul. I was exempted, and somehow, I ended up being the most broken one of all.

My mom's expression crumbles. She steps forward and brushes my face softly. "Oh, Topher."

CHAPTER 15

Katie

All around me, roulette wheels spin. The players watch with bated breath, tension and anticipation clinging to the air. Some bet on black, some bet on red. Some are hesitant, some are bold.

Casinos are the best place to prey on both the weak and powerful. They're all driven by one thing: greed, They all want to prove they can be better than the others. Some of them can't help but be controlled by the game, and some of them control the game.

This is only the third time I've ever been in a casino. The first time I came, I was eighteen and the night ended with me being groped by an old man. The second time, I put my foot down and refused to accompany Jamie, but he managed to convince me with a triple dare. This time, I came willingly. Anything to take my mind off him.

"Katie, it would be helpful if you didn't just stare all night. I can feel your eyes on my back. It's distracting," Jameson says without looking up from the cards in his hand.

I roll my eyes, fighting to urge to smack the back of his head. I could tell him that he's not going to win this round.

The eyes of the man in front of him brightened as soon as he received his cards. Then he went all in immediately. Everyone else folded, but not my friend. Jameson might think his ace of spades might earn him a victory, but no man bets everything he's got while wearing a ratty T-shirt and faded jeans. He's obviously not wealthy, which means he probably can't afford to lose.

My dumbass friend decked out in Tom Ford *can* afford to lose. Which is why I leave him to it. Not that I have much of a choice.

"I'm going to go get a drink," I state.

"Don't go too far," he says distractedly.

I get to my feet and head to the bar in the corner. The bartender smiles at me, waiting for my order.

"Sex on the Beach, please," I tell him.

He starts working on the drink while I look through my phone. There's one missed call from my dad and texts from my mom asking where I am. I moved back home a few days ago, and I guess I'm just tired. Of fighting with Dad, of pretending I know what I'm doing. If my actions a few days ago are any indication, I don't know anything. Except how to make mistakes, I seem to be a pro at that. I still can't believe Topher and I had sex without protection. He pulled out but that was way too close so I went to my doctor to get on the pill the following day.

I reply to my mom's text telling her I'm out with Jameson and I'll be home late. By then, my drink has been placed in front of me. I take a sip, looking around the casino and wondering what the hell I'm doing here. A guy moves to my side and smiles brightly. He's cute, with curly brown hair and a preppy outfit.

"You look like you need some company," he drawls, taking a seat beside me.

Not really.

"Hello to you too," I mutter, taking another sip.

He grins before nodding at the bartender. "I'll have a whiskey on the rocks. And I'll pay for whatever she's having."

"No thanks. I can pay for my own drinks," I tell him.

"But I want to pay. Come on, it's not every night I get to pay for a beautiful girl's drink. On the off chance that she'll spend the rest of her time talking to me."

He really is cute. My eyes meet his for a second. Blue, not brown. Even now I'm looking for something that reminds me of Topher. My gaze is pulled back to Jameson's table. He has gotten to his feet.

"Thanks for the offer and for paying for my drink. But I can't stay. Goodbye."

He doesn't follow as I head over to Jameson, whose eyes are narrowed in a glare at the other man.

"You cheated," he accuses.

I grit my teeth and look at the other guy, who seems to be growing angrier.

"You rich boys are all the same. What, is your ego bruised because you lost one little game?" he taunts.

Shit, shit. This could escalate at any moment. I step in front of Jameson, looking into his blue eyes.

"Jamie, let it go. It's not like you need the money. And you don't know for sure that he cheated. Just let it go."

He looks at me, a clouded expression on his face.

"Bullshit, Katherine. You weren't here. I saw him make a signal at the dealer. They're in on it together."

I turn around as the other guy rolls his eyes with a smirk on his face. He's baiting Jameson.

"Okay, okay," I say desperately. "Then let's just leave. Don't make a scene."

For a second, I think he's going to listen to me. Then he gently pulls me behind him.

"Stay back, Katie," Jameson whispers in my ear before stepping forward.

And then all hell breaks loose. Jameson throws the first punch. It hits Faded Jeans in the face and then he's throwing a punch of his own. The dealer gets involved and I yell frantically for someone to separate them. Most people just stare without moving closer. Then security arrives and once they're broken apart, I rush toward Jameson. He's bleeding from his nose and there's a rapidly forming bruise on the side of his eye. His lips have a cut, as well.

"You idiot!" I yell, punching him in the chest.

He winces. "Fuck, Katherine. That hurts."

I turn to the security men, who seem intent on having Jameson pay for the damages.

"How much does he owe?" I ask, because that's the quickest way to defuse this situation.

"Actually, the boss wants him brought in. He doesn't take kindly to people who accuse him of running a dirty game."

Oh, great. Jameson just had to open his big mouth and get us in trouble.

"Okay," I say, nodding while trying to think up a way out of this situation. "And who's the boss?"

"The casino belongs to the D'Angelo family."

My eyes widen and my blood runs cold.

"I'm sorry, what?"

I whirl around to face Jameson. He's staring at me with a guilty expression.

"This belongs to the D'Angelos?!"

"Calm down, Katie. It's one of the establishments they own under a fake name. I didn't think anything was going to happen."

A chill goes up my body. "Well, you thought wrong."

"It'll be fine. I'll go see him. Just wait for me outside, okay?" he says, placing a hand on my shoulder.

"Actually," one of the security men says, "boss wants to see her, too."

Oh, great. Just perfect.

"No," Jameson says. His jaw ticks as he moves to stand in front of me. "She's not going anywhere."

"You can come willingly. Or we can drag you there. Your choice, Mr. Clyde. But trust me, if the Don wants to see her, he'll see her."

He shifts slightly and my eyes are immediately trained on the glint of a gun in a holster at his side. I swallow softly as my heart rate speeds up.

"Let's go, Jamie."

We're led to a room at the back of the casino. I manage to surreptitiously send a text to my sister asking for help. She'll be able to track my phone's location. If anything goes wrong, she'll know where we are. One of the security men opens the door and we're ushered into the room. It's a dimly lit office, and seated at the table is Christian D'Angelo.

I've seen a lot of pictures of him. He's in his late twenties, with dark hair like Topher. They look alike, except where Topher's eyes are warm, there's nothing even remotely friendly about the man standing in front of me. He's attractive, with sharp features and a strong jawline. When he gets to his feet, it's easy to see that he's the man in control.

He walks toward us, gesturing at the couch in the office.

"Mr. Clyde, Ms. Malone, have a seat," he states.

There's something in the undertones of his voice that beckons obedience. He's a man used to being listened to. So we listen. Jameson and I sit down.

"I'm sorry about the fight. It was stupid of me and I promise I'll pay for all the damages," Jameson states.

Christian gives him a cool, appraising look, "Of course you'll pay for all the damages. Jameson, right?" he doesn't wait for a reply. "I won't take kindly to any more false accusations. Especially against our dealers. We run an honorable operation here, Mr. Clyde. If you lost, take it like a man, don't throw petty tantrums. They're beneath you."

Jameson's jaw is clenched but even he's not stupid enough to bait the head of a mafia organization.

"I understand."

"Good. Now, Ms. Malone." Christian turns to me. There's nothing in his expression that gives away what he's thinking. "You've been coming up on my radar quite a bit these past few weeks."

Christian leans against his desk and crosses his arms. "What's your relationship with my brother?"

"We don't have a relationship," I reply.

"Really?" He arches an eyebrow. "Because until a week ago, you were working for him, and you were photographed on a date."

"It wasn't a date. We were just hanging out."

"I thought you said you didn't have a relationship," Christian smirks.

"We don't. Anymore," I add quietly.

"Listen, Katherine, you seem like a nice girl. Smart, too. Topher's not great at making good decisions for himself, but I want to believe you're capable of that. I'm not going to interfere in whatever's going on between you two. And I'm not going to tell you to stay away from him, either. Just don't do anything that'll be detrimental to him. He's starting to find his place in the world. Don't jeopardize that. I'm asking for a favor here."

He sounds earnest, concerned. I can see just how much he cares for his brother. It actually causes a pang in my heart. The look in his eyes reminds me of the way Tessa looks at me.

"I won't do anything to hurt Topher."

I don't mention that I already have. Christian's about to say something else when there's a knock at the door. He calls for whoever it is to enter, and Carlo D'Angelo steps inside. I almost laugh—if my dad knew where I was right now, he'd lose his shit.

Carlo's eyes meet mine momentarily before he looks at his brother. He fires his next words in rapid Italian.

"What are you doing, Chris? Topher will lose his shit if he knows she's here."

"I was just making sure she understood some things," Christian drawls.

I understand every word they're saying, but I keep quiet. Carlo turns to Jameson and me.

"The two of you can go," he says in English.

"Don't forget what I said, Ms. Malone," Christian tells me.

We walk out of the office, but not before I hear Christian ask Carlo a question.

"They still haven't found her?"

I don't get to hear the reply before the door is slammed shut. We're ushered out of the casino and it isn't until I'm outside that I take an easy breath. I study Jameson's face. The bleeding's stopped but he still looks horrible.

He manages a smile. "Damn, Katie, I thought for sure we were toast."

I suck in a sharp breath. "Don't make jokes right now! You're the only reason we were even in that situation to begin with. What is wrong with you?"

"You can yell at me when we get home," he mutters.

I can tell he feels bad about what happened, but it's useless when he's continuously getting himself into situations like this. He could get seriously hurt. And a part of me believes that's what he's after. We're about to head over to the parking lot when a black Audi pulls up in front of us. My sister steps out of it and rushes over.

"Oh, god! I was so worried," she says, pulling me into a hug. She stares at Jamie for a second. "What the hell happened?"

Tessa insists on driving us, so we pile into our car. The ride is silent. She's obviously pissed, Jameson can't look her in the eye, and I'm still shaken from my conversation with the D'Angelos. We arrive at Jameson's apartment building, and I'm about to step out when Tessa stops me.

"Katherine, stay in the car. Jameson, out," she orders.

I stay put as she and Jameson exit. She moves to help him walk but he pushes her away gently. I watch as Jameson leans down to say something to her and she rolls her eyes. Her lips twitch like she's going to smile, but she doesn't. She places a hand on his arm and leads him inside.

I spend the next twenty minutes alternating between wondering who Topher's brothers are looking for to hoping my dad doesn't hear about tonight. News travels fast in this city. Christian's words keep eating at me. He said he wasn't telling me to stay away from Topher, but he might as well have.

It doesn't matter, though. I still remember the look on Topher's face as I walked out of his room. He wasn't angry, he was hurt. Despite how much he tried to hide it. I hate that I hurt him. And a part of me doesn't truly believe what he said.

Topher's the kind of guy to lash out when he's unsure of how to act. I'm almost sure he said what he said to get back at me. I refuse to believe he would use me like that. I'm the asshole in this situation. I did something wrong. He's probably the best thing that's happened to me in a while and I messed it up.

Tessa returns thirty minutes later. She lets out a shaky breath and I can tell she's a little rattled.

"I cleaned Jamie's wounds and put him in bed," she tells me.

"Alright," I say softly.

Whatever happened up there is none of my business. They're both adults. They'll figure their shit out.

Tessa takes a calming breath before looking at me. "What's going on with you, Katie? Talk to me."

"I quit my job," I confess. "It wasn't working out."

That's such an understatement, it's almost laughable. But I can't very well tell her that I slept with my boss, who also happens to be the son of our dad's mortal enemy.

Tessa frowns. "You're staying with me tonight."

"Won't your husband mind?"

"Kyle's away on a business trip," she replies. "You're coming with me. And you're going to tell me everything that's going on."

I lean into my seat and sigh. I know I don't really have much of a choice.

CHAPTER 16

Topher

"Are you fucking kidding me!" I shout as I barge into my brother's office.

I failed to take into account the fact that he might not be alone. The look Christian gives me is murderous and tension lines Carlo's face as he looks up at me. The police officer seated in front of them looks up at me, too.

His presence causes my eyebrows to rise. There are usually a few cops hanging around here, but none are ever so bold as to come in uniform. I can't help but wonder what business he has with the family.

"Topher, a knock next time would be ideal," Christian states, getting to his feet. The officer stands, as well. "Thank you, Officer Kane. Let me know if there are any other leads."

The officer shakes his hand before stepping out of the room. Christian flicks his gaze to me.

"I'm starting to consider revoking your access to the pub. I'll have someone inform me of your presence before you're allowed in here from now on," he says.

"Who was that?" I question, ignoring him.

Carlo sighs, crossing his arms and leaning further into the

couch. "You came to yell at us for meeting up with your girl-friend, so do it and go."

I look at both of them in turn. My anger dissipates at the sight of the worry on their faces. "What happened? You can tell me, come on," I press.

"You don't—"

"It's alright. He'll find out eventually," Christian says, looking at me. "Stacey's been abducted."

My eyes widen. "What do you mean abducted?"

"Kidnapped, Toph. She's gone," Carlo replies. "We got the call from her aunt a few weeks ago."

"Wasn't she supposed to be at law school?" I question, dumbfounded.

Stacey's relationship with our family is complicated. She's the daughter of the first man Christian had to kill. After her dad died, we couldn't turn our backs on her. Dad put her through school and made sure she had everything she needed. We've never really been close. I've seen her around, but she mostly stayed away from the three of us. Not that I blamed her. The last time I saw her was when she went to college.

"She passed her bar exam and was coming home the day she got kidnapped. From what we can gather, she made it to New York, but since then, nothing. There's been no news of where she could be."

I clench my jaw. No wonder they've been so worried. Especially Christian. Fuck, this must be eating at him.

"You think it's connected to the family?" I ask my brothers.

Christian shakes his head. "No. There's no trouble in the *Cosa Nostra* right now. There haven't been any demands and currently, there's no one acting maliciously toward me. It's been radio silent."

"There's a slight possibility she chose to disappear," Carlo says.

Christian glares at our eldest brother. "Why would she do that?"

"I'm just saying. You're so insistent on believing the worst-case scenario. Maybe Stacey's okay somewhere."

Christian doesn't say anything for several moments. I sigh softly. "I'm sorry," I say to both of them. "I didn't realize anything was up. I would have—"

Christian interrupts. "You would have what? Not spent the past few weeks gallivanting around the city with Katherine Malone? Stacey's case is about to be handed over to the FBI. Once they find out about her connection to our family, James Malone will get involved. Which means the situation's muddy as hell right now, Toph."

"I understand," I tell him with a nod. "I'll stay away from her."

Carlo gives me a look. "We're not forcing you to do anything, Topher." Christian rolls his eyes at that but my eldest brother continues. "If she's making you happy, we'll figure shit out on our own."

"No need. She and I don't have anything to do with each other anymore," I state.

"Really?" Christian drawls. "Because you looked ready to punch me a few minutes ago when you barged in here."

I shake my head. "That's nothing. Just stay away from her, Chris. I mean it, both of you."

"You got it," Christian states, moving behind his desk.

"Does *Mamma* know about Stacey?" I question.

Christian's eyes darken. "No, and you'll keep it that way."

"Understood. Just call me if you need anything."

He nods once. I ask him about Daniella and my nephew,

but it's pretty clear he wants to be alone right now. Carlo follows me as I step out of the office.

"Is he going to be okay?" I question.

Carlo rubs his jaw, staring forward. "You know Christian. He thinks everyone's his personal responsibility. It must be killing him that he wasn't able to protect her. Especially her."

"Who would do something like this, Lo? If they wanted to get back at us for something, I never would have thought Stacey would be their first choice. Only a few people know whose daughter she is and why she's so important to our family."

"Yeah, it's really concerning. Christian has called every Don and boss out there. When it didn't yield any answers, he turned to the police to see if their investigations had brought in any information. I honestly don't think it has anything to do with us. She could have been a victim of a random crime."

"Kidnapped by who? And why? If it's a kidnapping, we should have gotten a ransom call by now."

"Or she ran away with a boyfriend or something," Carlo mutters. "She could also be dead." His jaw tightens as he says the words.

He's already preparing himself for the worst-case scenario. And how Christian will react to it.

"You sure Chris will be able to handle that?"

"He will, because he's the Don and he's strong. But I know it'll hurt him a lot. He has Daniella, though. She'll get through to him."

I make the drive to the repair shop on autopilot. I can't stop imagining Stacey somewhere, chained up and terrified, or worse, dead. I didn't even know her that well but I'm worried regardless. Who knows what she's going through? And if I'm worried for her, then Christian must be going through hell right now.

Cara and Ellis are still hard at work as I walk through the open garage door. As soon as I do, Cara beelines toward me, a determined expression on her face.

"It's been a week," she starts and I arch an eyebrow, waiting for her to elaborate. "Katherine. She's been gone for more than a week. What happened? If you were going to fire her, the least you could have done was let me know."

Oh, I didn't realize I failed to inform them. Truth is, the past week, the mere thought of her felt like needles stabbing my chest. It hurt, and I hate that it hurt so I tried not to think about her at all.

"I didn't fire her. She left," I say tiredly.

"What do you mean, left?" Cara questions through narrowed eyes.

I shrug, "She quit, gave up, resigned—it's all the same thing, Cara. The point is she's gone."

"You could have told us. Instead of keeping quiet and making me question her absence all on my own, you could have told us she quit."

"She didn't give me an official resignation letter, so I didn't think there was a need for an official announcement."

"Don't play that with me right now, Topher," she says angrily. "I brought her here. I was the one that told her she could work here and then she just disappears."

"You know you could just pick up your phone and text her instead of bothering me, right?" I question, frowning.

"I tried but she's not replying to my texts. Something happened. And you need to tell me what."

I sigh. "I really don't feel like dealing with this right now, Cara. Later, okay?"

"Why? Because of that dumb magazine that had a picture of you two last week? Did you or did you not know her last name was Malone before hiring her to work here?"

"What's that supposed to mean?"

"I mean, it's kind of annoying that you're trying to turn your back on her now because of some bullshit rivalry your families have."

Something icy climbs up my chest. She doesn't know the full story, which is why she's throwing accusations like this, but it's really starting to piss me off. My eyes latch onto her green ones.

"I didn't fire Katherine and I never told her to stop coming here. We may have had a falling out," I say—understatement, "but if she's not coming to work, that's her decision. I don't really have any use for an employee that ditches her work without so much as a heads up, anyway."

It's cowardly and I hate it. I don't want to see her, and at the same time, I want to make sure she's okay. But whatever's going on isn't on me. She made a choice and she fucked up. I'm literally collateral damage.

Cara looks like she has something else to say but Ellis steps forward and places his hand on her shoulder.

"Hey, Car, you'd better check on that Buick again. There's some fluid leaking out of it."

He gives her a stern look. After a few seconds, she lets out a soft groan and walks away. His brown eyes meet mine.

"I'm not going to tell you how to run this place, boss, but Katie provided some much-needed extra help around here. Things were running smoothly for once."

My hand goes up to my hair and I pull softly in frustration. "I know. I'll figure it out."

"Alright." He moves closer and places a hand on my shoulder, his expression kind and warm. "Take care of yourself, Toph. You look like shit."

I arch an eyebrow. "What do you mean? I look impeccable as always, I'm sure," I say, my mouth curling up into a smile that feels entirely forced.

Ellis doesn't smile back. "Just take care of yourself."

That night as I'm leaving, I get a text from Katherine. Three words.

> Katherine: Can we talk?

For some reason, that makes me chuckle. The text feels like she's trying to sweep everything that happened between us under the rug, which is totally on brand for her. But I'm not about to give her an out like that. I'm tired of the back and forth between us. Christian was right, the last thing I should be doing right now is getting involved with her. Not now with everything that's going on with my family. I barely hesitate before texting her back.

> Me: Not interested, Katherine.

The worst part is, as soon as I send the text, a part of me wants to take the words back. Which is when I realize just how much I've started to care.

CHAPTER 17

Katie

I don't move when my bedroom door is opened. A few seconds later, the room is illuminated by light. With a sigh, I shift so I'm facing Jameson's, who is standing by the light switch with a frown on his face.

"I'm sure you don't need me to tell you you're being pathetic, right?"

A gasp flies out of my mouth. "What?"

"It's been two weeks, Katie. And the only thing you've done in those two weeks is lay around in bed, and watch some shows. You told your parents you were staying the night two weeks ago but clearly you moved back in. That's fine, you always have a place in my home but seeing you like this is sad and I can't watch it anymore."

My eyes narrow. "Wait, so let me get this straight. You spend the last two years on a path to destruction, and I watch and I let you do so because it seems like that's what you need. But when I spend two weeks in bed, it's pathetic? You asshole!" I yell.

He smirks, moving over to my bed. "You and I are not the same, Katherine."

133

"Whatever. Leave me alone, let me wallow in peace," I tell him, throwing my comforter over my head. "Also, could you get me some popcorn? I'm about to start binging *Gossip Girl.*"

I hear Jameson's soft sigh before he rips the blanket off my head. I glare.

"Dude!" I snap.

"Don't 'dude' me, you're a mess. So what if D'Angelo dumped you? Move on!"

I sputter, "That's—he didn't dump me. And this isn't about Topher, dammit! This is about the fact that my life is shit and I literally don't know what to do about it!"

"You can start by getting up."

"You choosing today to be sober doesn't mean I have to suffer along with you," I mutter.

He glares at that comment. "I'm not partying like that anymore. I quit after what happened at the casino the other day! And you would have noticed if you took time to pay attention instead of sulking like a fifteen-year-old."

That makes me sit up. "You're going to quit? Everything? The partying, the drinking, the drugs?"

"More or less," he replies, grinning. "All you need to know is that I'm done walking the path to destruction."

"Why?" I ask.

"Because I almost put you in danger. I realized I wasn't only harming myself with my behavior."

I study him for a few seconds. "That's not the only reason. What did you and Tessa talk about that day?"

"It's not something you need to concern yourself with, Katie. How about you? Did you tell her you slept with D'Angelo?" he questions, sitting on the bed beside me.

I shake my head. "She grilled me about it all night, but all I told her was that I was working for him, then I quit to appease Dad. If she found out I slept with him, she'd be pretty disappointed. Even she doesn't support me being anywhere near him."

"And yet…" Jameson says.

"And yet," I echo, shrugging. "Maybe they're right. I mean, it's probably a good idea to stay away from Topher. Not that it matters anymore considering he hates me now."

Jameson bumps his shoulder against mine. "He does not hate you. You rocked his world so hard that night, he probably can't stand to look at you anymore."

That makes me laugh. Jameson stares at me for a few seconds, long enough that it starts to make me uncomfortable.

"Why are you looking at me like that?"

"I'm trying to figure out how to help you."

"I don't want any help," I groan, throwing the blanket over my head. He rips it off again, and I sit up with a glare.

"I think you should see D'Angelo again," Jameson announces.

My look turns into one of disbelief.

"No, seriously. I think it might be good for you. If I'm being honest, I've never seen you happier than when you were with him."

"I wasn't *with* him," I say through gritted teeth.

"Alright, when you worked for him, then. You were happy and calmer, you found a sense of purpose. I think you need that again."

I don't say anything for several seconds, when I do, my voice is low and cold.

"He doesn't want to see me."

Jameson tilts his head to the side. "And you know that how?"

"Because I sent him a text asking to talk and he said no."

I'm still pissed about that. I sent it a few days ago in a

moment of weakness. A part of me wants to blame the wine I had drank. But there's the other part of me that can't deny that I sent it because I was thinking about him and because I missed him. When he told me he wasn't interested, it had hurt, more than he'll ever know.

That text is officially ranked very high on the list of the most embarrassing things I've ever done in my life. I wonder what Topher thinks of me now. Probably that I'm pathetic, like Jameson does. Something painful thuds in my chest.

"Okay, so he's going to need a little more convincing. It would be much better if you did it in person."

My eyes narrow onto his face. "What are you getting at?"

"I happen to know exactly where D'Angelo will be tonight. There's a party at the Playhouse. Topher knows the guy throwing it and I've got an invite."

"I thought you said you didn't party anymore," I say dryly.

"I said I wasn't going to be partying as hard anymore. I'm a twenty-three-year-old man, Katherine, you can't expect me not to go out at all."

"Alright. Have fun at your party, then," I tell him, waving him off.

"You're coming with me," he states.

"No, I'm not. Every single time you've dragged me out, I've ended up deeply regretting it. No more."

"I just want you to talk to D'Angelo. I promise we won't get into any trouble."

"There's no need."

"But there is. You obviously feel bad about how things went down between you two. So even if you're not going to get back together or whatever, the least you can do is have a conversation. Find closure so you can move on."

"Jameson," I say softly, looking into his determined green eyes. "Topher and I, it's never going to happen. It can't."

"We'll see."

THE LIGHTS in the club are dim as Jameson and I walk in. I finger the sleeve of my dress, torn between walking inside and running away. Like he can sense it, Jameson places his hand on the small of my back, guiding me forward.

"You said you would do this," he mutters.

"One of these days, we're going to have to conduct a study into your irritating ability to convince me to do things I don't want to."

He nods once, looking proud of himself. "Let me know how it goes."

We step into a room that's filled with bodies. The smell of alcohol and sweat clings to the air. The music is so loud my eardrums hurt. I get on my toes to talk to Jameson.

"I'm never going to find him in here!"

"He's probably in a VIP room in the back. Come on," he says, leading me through the people.

At least he hasn't ditched me yet. Someone taps his shoulder, gesturing for him to come over. Jameson tightens his jaw before refusing with a slight shake of his head. Pride rolls through me at that. Maybe he's finally changing.

We reach a part of the club that's quieter and I can finally hear myself think. Jameson stops a waiter, asking where Topher is, and we're led to a set of double doors. I silently hope he's not inside and we came here for nothing, but as soon as Jameson opens the door, my eyes meet his. My heart skips several beats. He's looking at me too, but my heart feels lodged in my throat when he looks away like I'm not worth his time. That look alone is enough to make me want to bolt. But Jameson practically pushes me into the room.

There are a few more people in here, all in various states of inebriation. Topher doesn't seem completely sober, either. There's a woman beside him on the couch, scantily dressed in booty shorts and a shirt that barely covers her tits. I don't know what she's whispering in his ear, but the sight of her hands on his chest causes something icy to slide up my veins. I move until I'm standing in front of them. It takes me a second to realize Jameson's not standing beside me anymore. I turn to find him in the corner of the room, having a conversation with another guy. He gives me a thumbs-up when he catches me staring.

I let out an uneasy breath.

"Topher, can I talk to you?" I question. He looks up at me, his expression blank and unassuming.

He doesn't reply, instead choosing to lean toward the table to pour himself a glass.

"Topher!" I snap when he continues to ignore me.

The girl beside him gets to her feet. She's much taller than me and her posture is confrontational, but I don't take a step back.

"You know, some of us girls have enough manners to know not to interrupt other people's conversations."

"Sorry, but are you done? I really need to talk to him," I retort.

She gasps softly before looking down at Topher, who is still ignoring me.

"Are you going to let her speak to me like that?" the girl snaps.

Topher takes a sip of his drink. "I don't control anything Katherine does, Colleen."

She stamps her leg onto the floor before walking away.

"You realize this is the second time you've cockblocked me, right?"

I roll my eyes before occupying the space Colleen vacated beside him.

"You can do so much better," I mutter.

"Really? And what's better? You?" he questions with a cruel smirk.

"You're drunk," I say, choosing to ignore his question.

"Thank you for the astute observation," he states dryly.

He leans back into the couch and some of his drink sloshes onto his chest. I grab the cup from his hand before he spills any more. Then he's looking at me, really looking at me.

"What are you doing here, princess?"

Something warm flickers in my chest at the sound of the nickname. I hadn't even realized how much I missed it.

"I came here for you."

"If you want me to have sex with you again to piss off your dad, you're out of luck. Getting used by women just doesn't appeal to me anymore."

I swallow softly. Okay, I deserved that. "I don't want to have sex with you again."

His eyebrows flick up. "Really?"

Before I can blink, his face is in front of mine and his hand is in my hair. My breath hitches at our proximity. Topher's breath is warm against my face. His mouth is impossibly close to mine and I find myself leaning closer, wanting to close the gap.

"You're a terrible liar," he says softly before leaning away.

It takes me a few seconds to regain my composure. "You have every right to be upset."

He fixes me with a dry look. "Thank you for granting me permission."

"No. That's not what I meant," I say in frustration.

His gaze flicks to mine and a slow smile pulls on the corner of his mouth. Warmth rushes beneath my skin, a prickling, breathless heat traveling down to my toes.

"You're pretty when you're all riled up. Color fills your cheeks and your eyes flare up, twinkling like stars."

I stare at him, uncomprehending. "What?"

"Nothing," he mutters. "I'm drunk."

"I could have told you that."

"Whatever. I'm going home." He gets to his feet only to end up stumbling backward. I quickly hold on to his arm.

He was speaking coherently; I hadn't realized he was this far gone. Topher leans against me and I quickly search for Jameson, who's already walking over.

"What do you need?" he questions, his green eyes flitting over Topher beside me.

"I'm going to take him home."

"You want me to come with you?"

I shake my head. "No, go home. I'll handle him."

He hesitates. "I didn't bring you here just to leave you alone with him, Katie."

"I'll be fine. Topher won't do anything to me, I promise."

He stares at us for a few more seconds before nodding. "Alright, fine."

"Go home, Jamie," I tell him seriously. I'm worried about what he'll get up to when I'm not here. He's on a good path and I'd hate to see him deviate from it because he was trying to help me.

He smiles. "Alright, Kitty Kat. I'll go home."

Jameson helps me lead Topher out of the club and toward

the parking lot. It takes a while to find Topher's black Mercedes.

"You sure you'll be alright?" Jameson questions and I nod.

"I'll be fine."

He leaves while I turn to Topher.

"I need your keys."

He shakes his head. "No one drives my baby."

"Come on, I promise I'll take good care of your precious car. I just need to get you home."

He stares at me for a few seconds without saying a word. Finally, he sighs, reaching into his pockets and handing me the key. I unlock the car and help him into the passenger seat before taking my seat behind the wheel.

Just when I think Topher's passed out, he turns his head and looks at me.

"Why did you seek me out? I was fine pretending you didn't exist."

"I hate playing pretend," I say tightly.

"Hmm. Of course you do, princess. When it comes to you, everything's real. And everything hurts."

I don't understand what he's trying to say. I concentrate on the drive and he doesn't say anything else until we're in his house. He lets me lead him toward his bedroom. I even help him out of his shirt and jeans, tucking him into bed. When I'm about to leave though, he grips my hand.

"I lied to you," he murmurs sleepily.

"About?" I ask, despite the racing of my heart.

It's all too much. Being in here with him is overwhelming.

"The worst thing I ever did wasn't sleeping with a married woman. It was when I almost beat a guy to death in college."

His hand drops away from mine at the end of that statement. He falls onto his pillow, and in a matter of seconds, he's
asleep. I don't move for several seconds as I take in his
confession.

Why did he tell me that?

CHAPTER 18

Topher

The smell of something burning propels me out of sleep and to my feet. Without pausing to think, I rush out of my room, heading toward the kitchen. My eyes meet panicked blue ones right before I jump into action.

"What the fuck, Katherine? Are you trying to burn the place down?" I put out the small fire on the stove by smacking it with an oven mitt. She's biting her lip with a frown. "What are you doing?"

Now that the fire's out, I take the time to let it sink in that she's here, in my house.

She sighs softly. "I was going to try to prepare us some breakfast."

I look into the pot, unable to even recognize what's inside or what she had been trying to cook.

"It looks more to me like you were trying to poison us both. Come on," I say, leading her out of the kitchen so she doesn't inhale too much of the smoke.

She falls onto my couch in a dramatic fashion and I raise

an eyebrow. Did we have some sort of reconciliation last night that's giving her reason to be so comfortable in here?

"I can't believe how hopeless I am in the kitchen. I was trying to poach eggs," she mutters.

Ah, so those were eggs. Damn. I almost smile at her abysmal attempt but I'm still confused as to her presence in here.

"I brought you home," she says, reading my expression. "You were pretty out of it last night."

My memory is a little hazy but I seem to remember her barging into the room at the club with Clyde.

"You didn't leave?"

"I slept on the couch," she replies.

"Why?"

"Because..." she trails off. "How much do you remember from last night?"

"I'm sure it'll all come back to me before the end of the day," I assure her.

She nods, looking distracted. I realize her eyes have trailed down to my body, around the same time I realize how little clothes I'm wearing.

"Take a picture, Katherine. I'll last longer."

She looks up at my eyes, a faint blush coloring her cheeks. Then she rolls her eyes.

"Go put on some clothes," she mutters.

I cross my arms over my chest. "It's not like it's anything you haven't seen before. Besides, you undressed me."

"Because I didn't want you to sleep with the smell of whiskey on your clothes."

"Solid excuse. But there's no way of knowing that you didn't take advantage of me in my inebriated state."

"Doubtful. I like my men sober," she says, repeating words I once said to her.

That makes me chuckle. "Sure you do. You also like men that are painfully oblivious to your true intentions while you fuck them."

Her breath catches and her expression falls. The sight almost makes me feel guilty. Almost.

"I'm going to go put some clothes on."

I head into my room. When I return, she's still seated on the couch. Her jaw is clenched and her hands are in her lap.

"I'm going to assume you sought me out yesterday because you had something to say," I begin, taking a seat. "I'm listening."

Her eyes narrow onto mine. "You have a right to be upset but you don't have to be a jerk."

"You'll find I excel at being a jerk, Katherine."

"You don't have to be a jerk to me," she retorts. There's something vulnerable in her expression. Something that gives me pause. "I just wanted to tell you I'm sorry. I never should have done what I did. I was in a bad place and I wanted to lash out. And you were the first person I thought of."

My hand goes up to my jaw. "Why? Why was I the first person you thought of?"

She ponders that question for a moment. Something flickers in her eyes before she shrugs. "Because you were the only person? It's not like I have a lot of people that could be in such a situation with me," she says coyly.

That's a lie.

"Say it plainly, princess. I was the only person readily available to sleep with you. Is that right?"

She swallows softly before nodding. "Yes."

I lean back into the chair. "In case you weren't aware, that does not make me feel better. You're not being honest, Katherine. I can count on one hand the number of times you've been honest with me."

145

"I-I don't know how," she says sincerely.

I can see it in her eyes. Katherine has built so many walls around herself. And a part of me really wants to find out why. Maybe if I knew the root cause of the problem, it would help me understand her better.

And more than anything, that's what I want.

"Okay," I finally say.

She looks at me in confusion, "Okay?"

"Yes, okay. I accept your apology. You could have thrown in some chocolates to sweeten the deal, but it's alright. You're forgiven."

"How benevolent of you," she says dryly.

I shrug, getting to my feet. "Just one rule, princess. If you ever want to sleep with me again, it had better be because you want to, with every fiber of your being. And not because you're being influenced by your father or anyone else."

Her eyes are on mine, firm and steady. "Deal."

TWENTY MINUTES LATER, I'm driving Katherine home because she's worried about her friend. On the way, she asks me how things are at the repair shop.

"I hired someone to replace you a few days ago. She's pretty good at her job. Annoys me a lot less than you do."

And she's infinitely less distracting, which I'm grateful for.

"She?" Katherine asks, her voice tight.

"Jealous?" I smirk.

"Of course not. It's better this way. It's not like I could work for you anymore. My dad would find out."

"Don't worry, princess. You'll always be my favorite employee."

"But I'm not your employee anymore. She hesitates. "So what are we?"

My lips curl into a smile. "I haven't heard that question since I was fifteen." I turn to look at her for a second. "We're friends, princess. Just like we were before."

"Being friends didn't work out so well the last time," she points out.

"No. But we'll do better this time."

"I'll hold you to that."

We arrive at Jameson's building. I don't say a word as she heads toward the stairs instead of using the elevators. She'll open up to me about it eventually. Katherine opens the door and I get the sense she's half-expecting us to find an orgy on the other side, like the last time. Instead, we find a shirtless Jameson walking around the apartment. He takes note of both of us with an arched eyebrow.

"Katie! You brought home a guest."

"Hey," she says uneasily. "How are you?"

"I'm good. Stop looking at me like that. I left the club as soon as you did. Came home, started *Gossip Girl* without you," he states with a smile.

"Asshole," Katherine retorts with a smile of her own.

I watch their interaction quietly, taking note of it. They're familiar with each other, the kind of familiar that honestly leans more toward platonic than anything else.

"Can we talk about him now?" Jameson asks, shooting me a pointed glance.

"Good to see you too, Clyde," I mutter.

"So, did you two make up? Get nasty beneath the sheets?" He waggles his eyebrows.

Katherine flushes. "Shut up, Jameson. That didn't happen!"

"Really? So what happened?" he asks curiously.

"Nothing."

"You didn't get back together?"

"We were never together. We're friends, Jamie."

He doesn't look convinced. "You sleep with all your friends?"

"For the love of God, Jamie!" Katherine shouts moving to stand between us. She pushes him backward.

"You tell him everything, princess?" I ask from behind her.

She whirls around to face me, biting her bottom lip. "He's my best friend."

"One that doesn't sleep with her," Jameson adds helpfully.

I laugh. He's persistent, I'll give him that. I walk around Katherine to face him.

"Katherine and I will take care of our own issues."

He doesn't look convinced. "Just to be clear, I'm the only person in her life that's actively pushing her toward you. Everyone else is telling her to run like hell."

"Why don't you?"

"Because I want her to find happiness that doesn't stem from her family's approval. She deserves at least that."

I smile. "I'm sorry for ever thinking you were a useless, waste-of-space friend."

He arches an eyebrow. "That's harsh, but I probably deserved it. We cool now?"

I slap his outstretched arm, "Sure."

We start walking toward the kitchen. "You hungry?" Jameson questions.

"As long as it's not something burnt, I'm in."

He chuckles. "She tried to cook, didn't she?"

"It was a disaster," I confirm.

The three of us settle down on the couch after breakfast to

watch their TV show. Which is around the time I remember everything that happened last night while I was drunk. It also hits me that I might have confessed my deepest, darkest secret to her. And she didn't run. I start to question her self-preservation instincts. I basically confirmed what she's always known, though.

Even before I could admit it to myself, Katherine astutely guessed that I was more like my family than I thought. I follow her into the kitchen when she starts to do the dishes.

"You know," I say.

She whirls around to face me. "What are you talking about?"

"When I was drunk. I told you about almost beating someone to death."

She sucks in a breath. "You don't have to talk about it if you don't want to."

I smile. "But you're curious. You want to know why."

"I don't need to know."

"Why not? You're worried, aren't you? That I'm not who you thought I was. That maybe you're wrong."

"I'm not wrong about you," she says assuredly.

"I'll tell you why I did it when you're ready to talk to me about elevators."

Her eyes narrow onto mine. "You'll be waiting a long time."

"That's alright, princess. I'm very patient."

CHAPTER 19

Katherine

I fall asleep to thoughts of Topher and the look in his eyes. A look that sometimes feels like it was specifically made for me. Thinking about him before I sleep is probably the reason for my dream.

I'm lying on my stomach, my cheeks pressed against my pillow, when I feel a voice in my hair. There's a hard length pressed against my ass.

He leans down to whisper in my ear, the words heated and dirty.

"I'm going to spank you so hard before I fuck you, princess. So fucking hard."

When his weight leans away, I push back against him to feel more. He says my name before turning me around. My eyes meet soft brown ones. His knees straddle my hips while his fingertips smooth along the sides of my breasts. Something hot and wet pools between my legs. Like he can tell, Topher smirks. His hand trails down to my panties and he shifts the fabric to the side before thrusting one finger into my pussy. I gasp softly, shamelessly rocking against him.

My hand fists in his hair. I pull him down and kiss him

hard, trying my hardest to imprint myself. Trying my hardest not to let go. Right before I wake up, he adds another finger and I climax, my mouth opening in a scream.

Reality pours over me like a bucket of ice. I teeter on the edge of waking, keeping my eyes shut. I can't believe that just happened. If Topher ever found out, he'd never let me live it down. Not that I'd ever tell him. His finding out that I'm having sex dreams about him will push us into a realm we're both trying our hardest to avoid.

Things are already complicated enough.

MY SISTER OPENS her front door, ushering me into her house with a grin.

"You're in a good mood," I note, taking a seat on the couch.

"Things are finally picking up. We got a collaboration deal with a designer in Paris. Mom and I will probably have to leave for a while, but it's such a good opportunity." She beams.

My chest feels hollow at that. If she and Mom leave the country, Dad will have no one to focus on but me. It honestly sounds like my worst nightmare.

"That's amazing, Tess," I tell her. "I'm proud of you."

"Thanks, Katie."

She talks for a little while about the designs she has in mind and the management of the business while they're gone, but I'm only half-listening. My thoughts have strayed to Topher. Tessa notices.

"What are you thinking about?"

"Nothing," I tell her.

Her eyes narrow. "You haven't contacted him again, have you?"

I look away. I hate that I have to lie to her, but Tessa hasn't made a secret of how much she despises the D'Angelo family. She's solidly behind Dad when it comes to matters concerning them. Which is why it hurts so much. Going against Dad is one thing, but my sister's the most important person to me. And I'm terrified that I might lose her trust.

"No, I haven't."

"You sure? Tell me the truth, Katherine. Because if you're still somehow involved with any of them, I need to know." She pauses. "Are they blackmailing you?"

"What? No."

"I just don't get why you started working for him, knowing who he is. Dad is still upset with you and Mom's worried every day that they'll somehow get to you and hurt you. It was dumb, Katie. Very dumb."

I know she means well, but her words sting.

"I'm sorry I'm not more like you," I mutter.

Tessa rears back, her blue eyes wide. "What's that supposed to mean?"

"It's true, isn't it?" I shrug. "If only I was more like you. The perfect daughter. The one that does every single fucking thing they want. Even at the expense of her own happiness."

As soon as I say the words, I want to take them back. Tessa doesn't deserve me lashing out. The way her expression crumples feels like a punch to my gut.

"I'm sorry. I didn't—"

"No, it's fine," she says sadly. "It's not like you're wrong."

"What's going on with you, Tess? You can tell me," I say softly.

There are tears in her eyes as she looks up at me. It's weird seeing that because my sister never cries. She never breaks—even during the worst moment of our lives. Even when it seemed like it was all over, Tessa was a boulder. She made sure to be strong for both of us. Which is why I hate disappointing her. The least I could do is try to survive on my own.

"I'm getting a divorce," she says flatly.

I try and fail to muster surprise. Tessa never married Kyle for love. She did it to appease Dad. Because at that time, all he wanted was an alliance with one of the most powerful families in New York. It was nothing more than a business transaction. Still, my heart shatters for my sister. It must kill her, those two years she spent shackled in a marriage she didn't want. My arms wrap around her.

"I'm sorry, Tessa. I'm so sorry."

She sniffs. "It's alright. I walked into this knowing that would be the eventual end. It hurts less when you know."

"Why did you do it if you knew?"

"Because I was stupid. Spineless. Because I would have done anything to make Dad happy. Because I wanted to protect you." I flinch at that. "I thought if I did anything he asked, he'd be less inclined to make your life harder."

My hands shake. "That's not right, Tessa. We shouldn't have to sacrifice our happiness for him."

"We're not," she says defensively. Try as we might, the truth is we're both Daddy's girls at heart. Deep down, we both know he's trying his best. He did everything to protect us. We would never turn our backs on him. "I didn't sacrifice my happiness. Kyle was a perfect gentleman. He made me smile, and a part of me actually did love him. Being with him was easy."

"Love is so complicated sometimes," I tell her.

153

Tessa laughs. "How would you know, Katie? You've never been in love."

I look away and sigh. "Maybe I haven't. But you have, and we both know it isn't with Kyle."

"No," she agrees, biting her bottom lip. "I started liking Jameson about three years ago. He took me to this party and I got really plastered, so he stayed with me throughout the night and even protected me from some assholes. I always knew he had a silly crush on me, but it was the first time I saw him as more than my little sister's best friend. After that, we started hanging out more. He would seek me out on campus, bring me flowers and gifts and other stuff."

"Wow. I must have been really stuck in my own world, because I had no idea."

"We were sneaky about it," Tessa says on a laugh. "Plus, we weren't dating. I thought he was too young. Three years doesn't seem like that much now, but when he was nineteen and I was twenty-two, it felt like a lot. He asked me out and I said no. I guess I was scared. Then I graduated and we didn't see each other for months. Until you invited him on that trip to Canada."

"When you got stuck together," I murmur.

"Yeah, and we had sex. It was amazing. But I felt awful after. Jameson noticed. He told me that if I was too much of a coward to face my own feelings then I probably didn't deserve him."

"Ouch, that's cold. But typical."

"Then his mom died and he just withdrew. I couldn't get through to him at all. Which is when Kyle came in. Dad actively pushed me toward him. Kyle seemed really into me and Dad's approval made me feel even better about it. I went along with it because it felt like the right path."

"You broke Jamie's heart," I say sadly. "And yours as well."

"I spent the past two years pretending it didn't matter. I thought I could ignore everything I felt. But it's hard to ignore how you really feel. Scratch that—it's impossible. Eventually, everything will build up until you can't ignore it anymore."

"So you're ending it with Kyle?"

She nods. "We'll sign the divorce papers before Mom and I go to Paris. I'll tell Dad when we get back."

That makes me smile. "Sounds like a great plan. That way he won't try to stop you."

"Yeah. Anyway, I told you all that so you'd stop thinking I'm so perfect. I make mistakes too, Katie."

Probably, but my mistakes are much bigger than hers. She couldn't bring herself to tell our dad about Jameson and Dad loves Jameson like a son. If he found out about Topher, he'd never be able to handle it. And what makes that knowledge worse is that my sister might not be able to handle it either.

A part of me knows that if it ever came down to it, she'd side with me. With what she's told me today, I know that at the very least, she'd understand where I'm coming from.

I head over to Topher's place after I leave, and he arrives about thirty minutes later. He doesn't notice me standing outside his door at first. His mind is clearly elsewhere and there's a pained look on his face. When he notices me, the expression vanishes and he smiles.

"Hey. I feel like I should just give you a key at this point, so you can let yourself in if you come around."

I nod. "That would be nice. Are you okay?"

"Yeah, I'm good," he replies, eyes light and playful. "What's up?"

He's great at shoving down his emotions.

"Nothing. I went to see my sister today. She's getting a divorce," I tell him as he opens the front door.

"That's rough, princess."

I follow him into the house and immediately take a seat on the couch, watching as he goes through the motions of taking off his jacket and turning on the lights. I study him for a moment.

"You know you can tell me if anything's wrong, right?"

Topher moves to sit down beside me on the couch. "What could possibly be wrong, Katie? Things are running smoothly at work and I get to see your beautiful face."

My breath catches. Then he makes matters worse when he leans closer to brush a few strands of hair from my face. I'm acutely aware of our proximity. I don't make a sound or make any movements, and he freezes when he realizes how still I am.

"What's going on in that head of yours?" he asks quietly.

I look up at him. Heat blooms beneath my skin and everything I want to say, everything I should say, gets caught in my throat. "You don't want to know."

His thumb trails down my cheek. "I want to know everything about you."

My traitorous eyes flicker down to his lips, every inch of me begging to close the gap. His gaze licks at my skin like fire as it trails along my face. I'm turned on by just the way he's looking at me. I wonder if he knows just how much power he has over me. Just how powerless I am when I'm around him.

"This is a bad idea," I murmur, inching closer despite myself.

Topher smiles. "Leap first, look later."

The statement barely registers. He leans in and kisses me. I freeze for a heartbeat, then my hand is in his hair as I deepen the kiss. My grip tightens on his clothes. Topher lifts me with barely any effort, placing me in his lap, right on top of his hard length. He wraps his arms around me, kissing me savagely. It's not slow and sweet, and it's not a kiss fueled by alcohol or because of my conflicted emotions.

It's a kiss born of desire so hot it threatens to burn me from the inside out.

I slide my fingers across his shoulders. One of his hands grips my hair, tugging hard, while the other reaches down to the hem of my shirt, dancing across my skin. I kiss him even harder. My fingers push through his hair, along the tendons of his neck. I'm about to rip his shirt open when a sharp ringing sound fills the air. I jerk away from Topher like I was caught doing something wrong. Which I probably was.

I'm still in his lap. He runs a hand through his hair, looking amused.

"You might want to get that, princess," he says, pointing at my bag in the corner of the living room.

I nod, still a little dazed as I get off his lap. My legs are a shaky when I get to my feet. My heart pounds with every step I take toward my bag. Jameson's name flashes across the screen of my phone, and I don't know if I should be irritated or pleased that he interrupted us. A part of me wants to ignore the call and continue where I left off with Topher. But I can't do that.

"What's up?" I ask, holding the phone up to my ear.

The voice that replies doesn't belong to my best friend, "You know Jameson Clyde?" the man questions, his voice rough and hard. I stiffen.

"He's my friend. What's going on? Where he is?"

"He's in a pretty bad way, sweetheart. Owes us some money. He said to call you so you'd bring it here."

Fear climbs up my throat. "Where is he?" I repeat.

157

A few seconds later, Jamie's voice is in my ear. He laughs nervously. "Hey, kitty Kat."

"Jamie," I breathe, "what's going on? Are you hurt?"

"I'm fine." The slight clench in his voice tells me he's anything but. "Listen, I need you to do me a favor. I got involved with some people a few months ago. And I forgot I was supposed to give them some money."

I groan, clenching my jaw. *Idiot. Idiot. Idiot.*

"How much?"

"Ten grand, cash," he replies, and my eyes widen.

"Where the hell am I supposed to get ten grand? I'm jobless, Jameson!" I yell, starting to panic.

Out of nowhere, the phone is snatched out of my hand. Topher starts to speak.

"Where are you?" he asks Jamie. When I open my mouth to tell him I would take care of it, he glares at me, a clear sign to shut up. I'm not sure what Jameson's reply is, but Topher nods. "We'll be there in twenty minutes."

He hangs up and barely glances at me before moving to his bedroom. I follow.

"Where are you going to get that kind of money so quickly?" I question.

He doesn't reply. I watch as he heads into his closet. A few seconds later, he's carrying a small safe. He inputs the passcode and I gasp when it opens. There's a lot of cash in there but that's not what surprises me.

Topher has guns. Three of them.

His jaw is clenched tight as he pulls out some of the cash. Then, as an afterthought, he grabs a gun as well. Another gasp escapes me. I don't think I'm breathing; my body feels hot and cold as I watch him move across the room, grabbing a bag to put the cash in.

"Katherine, wait here, okay?" he tells me.

That brings me back to reality. "What? No! I'm coming with you."

His eyes narrow. "I know exactly where Jameson is and I'm familiar with the people who have him. They're dangerous, okay? I need you to wait here for me while I go save your friend."

"He's my friend! And he called me asking for help. I'm going," I say stubbornly.

Topher looks like he's two seconds away from tying me to the bed.

"Please, I can't stay here. I'll be worried sick. Just let me come with you."

He takes note of the desperation in my eyes and nods once.

"Fine. Let's go."

CHAPTER 20

Topher

I send a text to Carlo on the way informing him about
the situation and asking for help. My hand clenches and
unclenches around the steering wheel as I drive with
Katherine silent beside me, her complexion pale and her eyes
wide and fearful. We arrive in front of the building fifteen
minutes later. She unhooks her seatbelt, her hand drifting
toward the door like she's actually going to follow me in. I
give her a look.

"Stay here, Katie."

"I can go with you. I don't know how badly hurt Jameson
is. You might need my help."

I take a deep breath, trying and failing not to get angry.
"You're staying in the car."

She gives me a stubborn look. "You can't make me. If you
leave me here, I'll just follow you."

"I'm trying to keep you safe!"

"And I'm trying to make sure nothing happens to either of
you. I'll be careful up there, I promise. I'll get Jameson and
I'll get out."

I close my eyes and take in another deep breath. "Their office is on the first floor, Katherine. Which means I need to take the elevator. Taking the stairs will take too long."

She shrinks back for a beat before a determined expression crosses her face. "I'll be fine."

"Katherine," I say, frustrated.

"We're wasting time arguing here. Let's just go."

She steps out of the car. She's right. Every second we spend out here is enough time for someone to put a bullet in Jameson's head. I step out of the car and stand in front of her.

"You stay behind me at all times," I tell her.

She nods, giving me a thumbs-up. We both head inside the building. At first look, it's a pharmaceutical company, but I know for a fact that the top floor is used for the more unsavory activities. They supply drugs to the top one percent of New York. They ship into the country in bulk, my family gets most of our drugs from here. The company's also known for providing hitmen on occasion, along with other violent activities. I'm not sure how Jameson got involved, but there's a huge possibility things could escalate.

Katherine stays by my side as we head to the elevator. No one stops us. I press the button to go up and a few seconds later, the doors open. There's no one inside it. I'm about to walk in when I notice Katherine hasn't moved. Her hands shake and she's staring inside blankly.

"You can stay here, princess," I tell her gruffly.

She seems to snap out of it, shaking her head. "It's just for a minute or two. I'll be fine."

A minute can sometimes feel like a lifetime. But I don't say that. She seems insistent on not letting me help her. She steps into the elevator, shutting her eyes as the doors close.

She's fine for the first few seconds, then she lets out a

shaky breath. Her entire body trembles. I shift closer, intertwining our fingers. She makes a soft noise before pressing her face against my chest, struggling with each breath. I don't think she's having a panic attack. She's just scared.

"I hate this so much," she chokes out.

"It's okay, princess," I say softly. "I'm here."

I run a hand through her hair, down her back. The gesture seems to soothe her a little. She takes in a steady breath. And another one, until her breaths start to even out. The elevator doors open and Katherine immediately takes a step back from me. I tense, reaching for the gun hidden under my shirt at my back, drawing comfort in the fact that it's still there.

They probably have him in the conference room. We pass a couple of people going about their business, men and women. Some of them handle the deliveries; some are in charge of roughing people up. Katherine dutifully stays behind me as we walk toward the room.

There are four men inside, and a woman seated at the table. She's dressed in a red jumpsuit, her dark hair falling across her shoulders. She's probably in charge. Katherine lets out a whimper when one of the men points a gun at my head as we walk in. My jaw grinds shut.

Jameson's in the corner of the room on the floor. His face is badly battered but otherwise he looks alright. He struggles to get to his feet, giving me a grim look. Regret flickers in his green eyes when he takes note of Katherine behind me. Once I'm sure he's not in any danger, I throw the bag filled with cash onto the table.

"Ten grand," I say to the woman. "It's all there. Now let him go."

She barks out a laugh. Her movements are slow and precise as she leans down into her chair and crosses her arms over her chest. "Hi, littlest D'Angelo. It's nice to meet you. I'm very acquainted with your brothers. My name's Maurine."

"Nice to meet you too," I say dryly. "Let my friend go."

She tsks, shaking her head. "You don't give orders. Topher, right? I've heard so much about you. Why don't you stay and play with me for a little while?" Her eyes gleam as she stares at me. "Your girlfriend can join, too."

My hands curl into fists. "No thanks."

"Really? That's too bad," she says on a soft sigh. "Jameson was just getting comfortable. Isn't that right, Jamie?"

He doesn't reply.

Maurine smiles. "I'd hate to let the three of you go just like that. It seems so boring."

One of the men advances on me and holds me down. My eyes widen when another grabs Katherine's wrist. Jameson rushes forward. I don't even hesitate—I jam my elbow into the gut of the guy holding me before grabbing my gun and pointing it at the man gripping Katherine's arm.

"Let her go. Now," I order, my voice deceptively calm.

He does, backing away slowly. Maurine laughs. "So the littlest D'Angelo has claws as well. That's good to know. I'm curious, though, would you really shoot?"

In a flash, a gun is being pointed at Katherine's head. My eyes widen.

"If I asked Acid to shoot, he would. Without hesitation. Would you shoot without hesitation as well?"

"I will shoot every fucking person you know if you don't tell your puppet to drop that fucking gun," I say quickly pointing the gun at Maurine.

My lungs burn as I take in the impossible situation in

front of me. Katherine's eyes meet mine, steady and bright. She trusts me; she's trying to communicate to me that she understands. She swallows softly, and I know that despite her outward appearance, she must be scared out of her mind. A tremor goes through my hand as it moves to the trigger. The tension in the room could be cut by a knife. Then a phone rings and it seems to dissipate marginally.

"Hello," Maurine sings, answering her phone. "Oh, Christian. How interesting that you called me. Your brother's right in front of me right now."

She falls silent as Christian responds. Then she laughs. "Of course I didn't hurt him. I'd hate to be the recipient of that notorious D'Angelo wrath I've heard so much about. Besides, I'm the one in danger here. The fucker's got a gun pointed right at my head and something tells me he's not a bad shot." She says then listens to something else he says before sighing. "Fine, I guess I have to let him go. Bye, Christian. I look forward to our next transaction."

She hangs up and gets to her feet. The man holding the gun to Katherine's head drops it. I keep mine up as I move to stand in front of her.

"Oh, calm down. You're the don's kid brother you think I'd kill ya? Your big brother told me to leave you alone. Although he threatened me with a few more colorful words. You can put the gun down now."

I arch an eyebrow.

"I'm sure he did," I say flatly.

She reaches forward and places a hand on my jaw, stroking it gently. "Tell your friend not to make promises he can't keep, okay? We're not fond of people who break promises."

"I'll make sure he understands that."

"Alright. You can go. Until we meet again, littlest D'Angelo."

Jameson walks over and Katherine immediately wraps her arm around his, helping him stand on his feet. They walk out of the room and I follow, pausing to hide my gun under my shirt again. I help Katherine get Jameson to the elevator. She seems too shaken by what happened to have another panic attack, which I'm grateful for.

It isn't until we're out of the building that I take my first full breath. Then I'm looking into Jameson's green eyes.

"I would punch you if you weren't already a mess," I tell him with a glare.

He nods, his expression sober. "I deserve that. I'm sorry. I just didn't have anyone else to call."

"What would have happened if I hadn't come? What did you think she would have done?"

"I'm sorry," he says, hanging his head guiltily.

Katherine places her hand on my arm. "It's fine. I'm okay. We're okay."

I look away, staring into the distance. I can't stop thinking about what happened a few moments before. My heart went into overdrive the moment she was in danger, and it's still pounding in my chest.

"We should get Jameson to the hospital," Katie murmurs.

He shakes his head. "No, please just drop me off at home. I'll be fine."

"But you need to get checked out," she argues.

"I'll be fine, Katie. You wouldn't mind staying at his house tonight, right? I'm sorry, but I really can't look at you right now without feeling like a total piece of shit."

"I'm not going to leave you alone," Katherine says stubbornly.

"I'll call Tessa."

She's a little appeased by that. "You can't tell her about Topher or what happened."

"I'm not stupid, Katie."

She nods, helping him into the backseat of the car before turning to face me.

"If I wasn't with you, what would you have done?" I ask. The thought of her going up there alone literally causes my heart to hurt.

She shrugs. "Anything to save him."

My eyes roam across her face. "That's what I thought. Let's go."

After dropping Jameson off, I take us both to my house. Katherine curls up on the couch as soon as we're inside. I watch her for several minutes, unmoving. I can feel the slight shift in the air. The shock of what happened starts to dissipate, leaving only the weight of what went down today.

"I half-expected you to go to your parents' house," I say, breaking the silence.

She looks up at me sharply. "Why would I do that when I can stay here with you?"

That gives me pause. I lean against the wall and stare at her. "Katherine," I say, then stop because I really don't know where to start. Our kiss earlier, what happened when we rescued Jameson—so much has happened in so little time.

Katherine takes in a deep breath before speaking. "Were you actually going to shoot her?"

I can't read the expression on her face. But I give her an honest answer regardless.

"I don't know."

She nods like she was expecting that. "Why do you keep guns?"

There's only one answer to that. "Because I'm a D'Angelo."

"Have you ever…" She pauses and looks away before her eyes find mine again. "Have you ever killed anyone before?"

"No, I told you I haven't. I came close once, though," I say.

"What happened?"

"What happened when we were in the elevator?" I retort.

She looks away.

"You can't expect me to bare my heart and soul to you, princess, and not reciprocate. That's not how it works."

"I know," she tells me softly.

"So talk to me."

She gestures for me to come closer. I hadn't even realized I was standing so far away. I guess a part of me was worried she wouldn't want to be near me anymore, not after she saw me battling the urge to shoot someone. As soon as I sit down beside her, she leans into me, seeking my warmth. I let out a soft breath of relief and wrap my arms around her.

"I have a fear of enclosed places. Claustrophobia," she mutters.

"Yeah, I figured," I tell her.

"I didn't always have it. It started when I was sixteen."

"Why? What happened?" I squeeze her arm gently, trying to convey to her that she can trust me.

"My sister and I were kidnapped. You know my dad's the director of the FBI but back then he was a regular agent. He had just closed a case involving a serial killer and things were relatively quiet. Until he started getting death threats from someone. Promises to destroy him and his family. They were later traced to a man named Charles Leeman. He was the serial killer's younger brother."

Katherine pauses to shift closer to me, and my grip around her tightens. When she shivers, I run a hand through her hair to soothe her.

"Charles grew obsessive after his brother was locked up. My dad wouldn't let any of us out of his sight for so long. Tessa was in her second year of college. She had to have someone tailing her at all times, for her own protection. The threats continued for a week, but we were never allowed to see any of the letters so Tessa and I didn't know how bad it was. We weren't oblivious, we just didn't realize it was that serious. She came home one day after ditching her body-guard. She wasn't as serious then as she is now. I guess the experience changed her a lot." She pauses like she doesn't want to say any more.

"Keep going," I prompt gently.

"Tessa came home and managed to convince me to sneak out to a concert with her. It was supposed to be a few hours. Mom and Dad weren't home; if they were they wouldn't have let us. I guess we were both tired of constantly being watched. When we were driving back home, though, our car got a flat tire. Tessa stepped out to check it out and the next thing I knew, I was hearing her scream. I rushed out of the car and I guess I got hit in the back of the head because I passed out. When we woke up, we were in a basement. A really small basement."

My breath hitches. It's all starting to make sense to me. Katherine's voice is strong as she relays the rest of the story.

"He fed us once a day. Every day, he would open the door and bring us some food. It was always dark so we never really saw his face. It was terrifying. Tessa would hold me and sing to me and tell me to be brave. She made so many promises to keep me safe, to protect me. She promised me that we weren't going to die in that basement. We were in there for three days. He kept us hidden pretty well. He wasn't stupid enough to get caught, and we realized we had to escape on our own. On the fourth day when he brought us some food, Tessa jammed a piece of wood into his leg. It worked momentarily. He went down in pain and we started racing up the stairs. But then—" She stops, her breath catching. "He caught her. I turned around and saw my sister get slammed down onto the stairs. I didn't move but then Tessa was yelling at me to go. He pulled her to his side and held a knife to her and told me that if I left, he would kill her. But Tessa was insistent that I leave. She told me she'd never forgive me if I stayed behind. So I left."

It takes me a moment to realize she's crying softly. I tilt her head back and brush some of the tears away.

"Hey, that wasn't your fault. You were strong, and you knew you had to survive."

"He stabbed her, Toph. I got out and I got help, but by the time the cops got there, Tessa was almost dead. He was gone. They almost didn't get him, but eventually, he was apprehended. Tessa was unconscious for almost a week. It was honestly worse than the time I was abducted. I was going crazy from the grief and the guilt. I would have never forgiven myself if she didn't wake up."

"She wouldn't have wanted you to feel like that."

"I know. I spent almost two years in therapy unpacking everything. Tessa only got therapy for a year and she was okay. I'm the one that became claustrophobic. She was the one that suffered the most and yet I'm the one still broken from what happened."

"You're not broken," I say fiercely. "You're just as strong as your sister. You experienced something traumatic; you were starved and terrified and yet you made sure to go back there. You saved her just as much as she saved you."

She smiles softly. "You sound like my therapist."

"Really? Must have been a good one."

She laughs and a smile pulls on my lips. Sometimes I

want to bottle up the sound of her laughter and carry it with me everywhere I go. It's starting to dawn on me just how deep my feelings for her have become. But I don't say that yet.

"I'm getting better, though," she says, like she has something to prove. "Before, I couldn't go on trains and I couldn't be left alone in my own bedroom for too long. Mom had to sleep with me for months." She laughs softly. "It was pretty rough the first couple of years."

"I understand, princess," I tell her, my thumb brushing across her cheek. "Please tell me the asshole's dead."

She shakes her head. "He was sentenced to twelve years for forced imprisonment, kidnapping, and attempted murder."

"Twelve measly years?" I say dryly.

She shrugs. "He got the judge to be sympathetic, I guess. It also helped that he had no former convictions. He was a first-time offender. A normal guy, until his brother went to jail."

My jaw clenches. Katherine reaches up to smooth it over.

"Hey, it's okay. He's locked up. He can't hurt me anymore."

I raise an eyebrow. "Shouldn't that be my line?"

She grins, right before she yawns softly. "I'm just going to shut my eyes for a couple of seconds. Then you can tell me your story."

Her head is on my chest and a couple of seconds turns into minutes and then she's just fast asleep. Not that I blame her; after the events of the day I'd be exhausted as well. Except I don't sleep easily, and I suspect I'll be kept awake for a relatively long time.

I carry Katherine into my bedroom and place her on the bed. Her blonde hair fans out on the pillow, and my chest feels heavy as I take in her soft expression.

For the first time, I fully understand how Christian feels. The desire to protect things that belong to him. Something visceral and painful slashes across my chest at the thought of Katherine being hurt.

I realize that I made her mine without even realizing it. And it honestly feels like I've damned us both.

CHAPTER 21

Katie

My eyes fly open and immediately land on soft brown ones.

"Watching someone while they sleep is creepy, Toph," I mutter, sitting up.

"You're so pretty. I could watch you all the time," he says sincerely.

I flush, my chest growing ridiculously warm. "What time is it?"

"Ten p.m. You were asleep for three hours," he informs me.

It's not surprising. I was emotionally drained and stressed. "I have to pee," I mutter, needing to get away from the intense look in his eyes.

He nods. "I'll be in the kitchen."

He heads out of the room, giving me time enough time to pull myself together. When I step outside, he's at the kitchen counter, pouring green liquid from the blender into two glasses. I make a face.

"Please tell me you don't expect me to drink that," I say.

"It'll help calm you down. It's my mom's secret recipe," he says with a wink.

He hands a glass to me and I gag. "Topher," I cry, staring at the cup.

He grins before consuming the contents of his glass in one gulp. "I promise it's not that bad," he says after.

I'm not inclined to believe him, but he continues to stare at me expectantly so I take a sip. When I realize it really isn't too bad, I drink some more before setting it down on the counter. "Yeah, I'm done."

He shakes his head before grabbing both cups and rinsing them out and putting them back into the cupboard. He's neat and tidy, which is at odds with his personality. Right when I think I have him all figured out, he surprises me.

Topher moves forward and grabs me by the hips to set me on the island. I let out a squeal of surprise. He steps in between my spread legs and slides his hands up the sides of my thighs. The warmth makes me shiver, and I recognize the hungry look in his eyes. I'm sure it's mirrored in mine, but I also refuse to be distracted.

"I told you my truth. Now it's time to tell me yours," I tell him.

He sighs, his head dropping against mine. "Do I have to?"

"Yes," I say on a laugh.

"What if it changes how you see me? What if you don't want me anymore?"

The question is raw and vulnerable. It doesn't surprise me that he knows how much I want him. I've wanted him from the first moment I met him. I place my hands on his jaw, lifting his head so he's looking me in the eye.

"Nothing would ever change how I see you," I promise. "Just tell me."

He offers me a small, distracted smile. His hand is still on my hip, I can feel him drawing little circles over and over again.

"I was in my second year of college, and there was this girl I was hanging out with at the time. We weren't dating or anything like that. We were merely friendly since she was in most of my classes. Anyway, she got assaulted at a party, and when I found out who did it, I just lost it, I guess. I got my hands on a hockey stick and beat him so badly that he lost consciousness. I probably wouldn't have stopped, but some people pulled me off him."

He doesn't look at me as he speaks, but I can see in his eyes that he's ashamed. He hates that he did it.

"Everyone makes mistakes, Toph," I tell him softly.

"That wasn't a mistake. I almost lost myself that day. My dad always used to say that the first kill is the hardest. After that first kill, everyone else becomes blurred. You lose yourself and it becomes so much easier to take a life. It scared me after I beat the kid up because I realized I would be toeing an edge for the rest of my life. One small slip-up and it would all be over. You were right when you told me I was just like the rest of my family. I guess I've just always been scared to see that."

"There's no clear edge, Topher. Life isn't just black and white. There aren't any good or bad people. My dad has killed before, and that hasn't changed him. It doesn't make him a bad person."

"No, it just makes him a controlling narcissist," Topher mutters.

I glare at him and he offers an apologetic smile. "Okay, fine. Look at your brothers, I don't think they're inherently bad people."

Topher snorts. "Trust me, princess, they're bad people. Just not to the people they care about."

"Exactly. That's my point, there's no clear edge. Even if one day you find yourself in an impossible situation where you have no choice but to pull the trigger, it wouldn't change you."

"You can't know that for sure, *cuore mio*," he says softly.

"I can and I do," I say confidently. "I see you, Topher. All of you."

"Yeah. I know you do."

He pulls me even closer to his body, and I shiver when he leans down to suck a sensitive spot behind my ear. My entire body melts at his touch. His erect cock presses against my clit, making me gasp softly.

"If you don't want me to kiss you, you'd better tell me now," Topher murmurs against my skin.

I remember what he told me a while ago so I shift away to look him in the eye.

"I want you. I want to kiss you and have sex with you and it has nothing to do with my family. There's no hesitation, no hidden agenda, I just want you, Topher."

He smiles. "That sounds perfect, princess."

He makes a rough noise before picking me up. I wrap my legs around his waist and rest my face on his neck as he carries me into the bedroom. I slide down to the floor and remain still in front of him, my breathing erratic.

He still hasn't kissed me yet, and my heart is literally pounding in expectation. His hands slide down to my waist, my hips, skimming the outsides of my thighs. The caress is slow, reverent, like he's trying to memorize the curves of my body. Heat blooms beneath my skin, tightening in my breasts and burning lower.

Topher's gaze is possessive as he looks at me.

He makes a short sound of satisfaction before pressing two of his fingers against my core.

"You're so hot and wet for me, baby," he whispers.

Standing up on my toes, I skim my lips against his, waiting eagerly for his mouth to claim mine. Topher grasps me by the throat, pushing me back against the edge of the bed. An explosion of fire bursts inside of me when he finally kisses me. My blood sizzles and every inch of me tingles. The press of his mouth against mine hits me with intensity.

I gasp softly when he nips at my bottom lip. Then he licks it, soothing away the sharp sting with his tongue. A moan escapes my throat and my fingers curl. I scrape my nails down his stomach, stopping at his belt buckle. My hand presses against his hard erection and heat unfurls in my belly. I want to know what he tastes like. I want so badly to drive him wild.

Topher's eyes widen when I drop down to my knees, and heat flares in his gaze. He realizes what I'm about to do. I rub my hand against his hard, thick length, and he lets out a soft breath. I can feel his gaze on me as I work on his pants, pulling them down as well as his boxers. As soon as I do, his cock bobs in front of me. I look up and find his eyes fixed on me, darkened with pleasure. He doesn't make a sound as he watches me wrap my hand around his shaft, but he groans softly when I lean forward to lick the tip.

I run my tongue across his crown before sliding him into my mouth. I gag softly when he hits the back of my throat, sliding him back out only to repeat it again and again. Topher's hand caresses my neck. The movement causes a raw wave of warmth to flicker in my chest.

Topher slowly slides in further. I take as much of him as I can before releasing him with a loud pop. My hands wrap around him, thrusting up and down. When I reach for his balls, he lets out a soft moan.

"I'm going to come, princess," he tells me.

I blink up at him in acknowledgment, and a groan rumbles from the back of my throat as he finishes in my mouth. I swallow every last drop, my cheeks heating under the weight of his stare. Topher runs a thumb across my bottom lip before lifting me to my feet.

"Kiss me," I whisper softly, needing something to distract me from the feeling in my chest.

My heart burns when he does. Grabbing the back of my neck, he presses his mouth to mine, our tongues sliding against each other. A deep, empty ache pulses between my thighs. Topher moves his lips to my neck and lets out a rough sound when his hand slides between my legs. He shoves my thong to the side and my mouth drops open when she pushes two fingers inside of me. A flush warms my body as I writhe and pant under his touch. Each time he slides his fingers inside of me, I feel myself lose another inch of my control. Until I'm completely and utterly at his mercy.

"That's it, Katherine. Feel everything."

"Topher, please," I beg. I don't know what I'm asking for. For him to stop or for him to never stop.

My orgasm hits me hard and I feel my eyes roll to the back of my head. Air is knocked out of my lungs. When I finally come to, Topher's above me on the bed. He smiles softly, brushing some of my hair out of my face.

"You realize I'm never letting you go after this, right?" he questions.

"I can live with that."

His hand tightens around mine. "Promise?"

"Pinkie," I tell him. He grins before kissing me again, each slide of his tongue against mine more perfect than the last.

Topher only lets me go so he can reach for a condom in his bedside table. He fucks me missionary, the two of us staring into each other's eyes as he thrusts into me. It's slow and sweet and leaves me feeling full and drained at the same time. He whispers the word "mine" so many times over, it feels like an imprint against my chest. We come together and I lie down beside him, kissing his jawline, his cheeks, his lips.

I spent such a long time hiding from how I felt, and now, in this moment, it almost feels like I'll explode if I continue to keep it all in.

MY HEAD IS on Topher's chest as we watch *Gossip Girl* in silence. We've spent the entire day together, lying in bed, ignoring the rest of the world, having sex. It's the most fun I've had in a long time. His hand trails down my arm absent-mindedly. I'm trying to concentrate on the show but it's distracting, making me acutely aware of his presence. When I look up at him, the smile on his face tells me he's been doing it intentionally.

I glare before shoving off him. "I'm going to get a drink," I tell him.

"Bring me some juice?" he asks and I nod. "Thanks, princess."

I'm halfway to the kitchen when someone rings the door-bell. Topher's eyes flick over to mine and he tenses. Whoever it is has effectively popped the bubble we tried so carefully craft around us. He walks over to the door and opens it.

"Hey, *fratello*," Topher greets, barring the doorway.

"So you're alive." I hear Christian D'Angelo's dry voice. "Good to know. Although a call would have been much appreciated."

"I'm sorry. I was going to talk to you tomorrow."

Christian makes a small noise of annoyance. A part of me

hopes he'll leave, but then there's the sound of a child giggling and a woman's voice in the air.

"Would you move from the door?" she asks, pushing past Topher and into the house.

I take her in slowly, the baby in her arms and the expression on her face. Her blue eyes widen as they meet mine. Then she whirls around to face Topher.

"I told you they were dating!" she says excitedly.

I just stare, confused at the situation. Topher sighs as his brother steps in and shuts the door.

"Yes, *tesoro*. I'm so glad you were proven right," Christian says, sarcasm lacing his words.

She frowns, moving toward me. "Hi, I'm Daniella. Christian's wife. You're Katherine, right? It's so nice to meet you."

I shake her hand, a little dazed. The energy around her is a little overwhelming.

"Nice to meet you, too."

Her baby reaches forward to touch my hair. He giggles, his brown eyes practically gleaming as he plays with it. I immediately soften, reaching for his hand. He clasps my thumb and something melts in my chest. I've always loved kids.

"Hey, little guy," I say softly.

"His name's Daniel," Daniella informs me.

I look up at her with an arched eyebrow and she lets out a soft sigh.

"I know what you're thinking. At the time, it seemed like such a great idea to name him after me, but now we spend every day regretting it because it's so confusing."

"Speak for yourself," her husband rumbles from the couch.

He and Topher are discussing something in hushed tones. I'm almost positive it has to do with our little adventure yesterday. Topher looks at me once and I feel the heat simmering in his expression down to my toes. Daniella notes it with a smile.

"You have no idea how happy I am the two of you got together," she states.

"Thank you?" I say, wondering why she's so happy considering the situation with my dad.

"I might not know you but I know you make Topher happy. He's family and I want him to be happy. Plus, he's matured a lot since he met you. I know the thing with your dad is a bit much but who knows, maybe the two of you can settle this ongoing rivalry within our families."

"Well, it's not really rivalry. My dad's job is to uphold the law and the D'Angelo family runs a criminal empire so it's a little more complicated than that," I say on a laugh.

"I can hear you, princess."

He moves behind me, his hand landing on my hip as he looks at his sister-in-law.

"You're being a meddler. How would you have liked it if I meddled in your relationship?" he questions, his eyebrows raised.

Daniella rolls her eyes. "You did meddle and you were annoying."

"I definitely don't remember that."

"Whatever. Could you hold Dan for a while?" she asks, placing the baby in my hands. "I'll go make us some refreshments."

"You're staying?" Topher asks, sounding annoyed.

"Yep."

Daniella walks over to the kitchen while I head to the couch and take a seat. Far away from the brooding man with cold brown eyes. Christian smirks as he watches me.

"I had a conversation with your father yesterday," he

starts, making my eyes widen. "He accused me of trying to corrupt his daughter."

"I'm sorry about that," I mutter.

"It's alright. I just find it interesting that he doesn't seem to be aware of this little situation."

Topher places a hand on my shoulder. "The situation's fairly new, Chris. Lay off."

"So you're going to keep it hidden?" he asks dryly. "For how long? He'll find out eventually. I'm actually curious about who she'll pick. It's not easy to turn away from family."

My jaw clenches as I look down at Daniel's chubby baby cheeks.

"I won't turn away from my family," I say determinedly.

"That's admirable. But eventually, you're going to have to choose. Deep down, you know it, too."

I glare at him. He doesn't have to be such a jerk. I was so happy before he walked in here with his blunt remarks.

"Christian," Topher says through gritted teeth.

He smiles. "What? I might as well prepare you guys for it. For what it's worth, though, I sympathize with you. It won't be an easy choice to make."

He grabs his phone, seemingly done with the conversation. Topher gives me a tired look before moving to sit beside his brother. We watch the show silently for a few minutes before Topher asks Christian something quietly.

"Any news on Stacey?"

I have no idea who Stacey is, but Christian's jaw goes tight. "I would tell you if there was, Toph."

He nods. "Alright."

Daniella returns and the tension dissipates. She sits next to her husband and we spend the rest of the evening together. I never would have thought I would find peace with the

D'Angelos. I think about what Christian said about me having to choose.

Even thinking about it feels like a betrayal. But one evening with them made me see them for who they are. Even Christian isn't the monster I always thought he was. I realize that a life with Topher would be amazing but how would that ever work? I can feel him tugging on every part of my being but what about my family? I doubt I could ever turn my back on them.

CHAPTER 22

Topher

I feel the shift in the air as soon as Christian and Daniella leave. Katherine's still seated on the couch, but there's a far-off expression on her face that eats at me. I take a seat beside her and throw my arm over her shoulder. She tries to push me off but I don't budge.

"What's with the frown on that beautiful face?" I ask softly.

She rolls her eyes, although her cheeks redden a little. "Nothing," she mumbles.

"Liar. You're thinking about what Chris said. It's bothering you."

"He made some solid points," she says quietly.

I turn her so she's facing me, "Christian's an ass. Don't let whatever he said get to you."

"You know we still need to have a conversation, right? We can't just pretend our problems away."

I sigh and lean on her shoulder. "Why can't we?"

"Topher…"

"Alright, fine," I state, looking up. "Obviously, we need

183

to keep our relationship a secret, especially considering how bad things are right now."

"Bad? Something's going on, isn't it? A few weeks ago when I talked to your brothers at the casino, I overheard them talking about finding someone. And then today you mentioned Stacey. Who is she? What's going on?"

I consider the implications of telling her the truth. There's a slight possibility hearing about what happened to Stacey might trigger some of her traumatic memories. But looking at the expectant expression on her face, I know I can't keep it from her.

"Stacey's a friend of the family," I say slowly. "She went missing a couple of weeks ago. We haven't heard anything since."

Katherine pales. "What? Who took her?"

"We don't know. The last time I asked, her case was handed over to the FBI. Which probably explains how your dad and Chris had a conversation. I guess he's paying attention because it concerns our family."

"Or he's probably paying more attention because it reminds him of what happened to my sister and me," she says softly. "Oh my god, Toph, I'm so sorry. Are you okay?"

"I'm fine. Christian's having it much worse. I didn't know Stacey all that well," I tell her, rubbing her shoulder. "But things are pretty tense right now."

"Yeah, if my dad found out about us now, he'd probably blow up and have me shipped to Antarctica."

I make a face at that. "You know you don't have to do everything he says, right? He's your father, but you're a full-grown adult. He doesn't own you."

"Remember when you told me to keep my biased opinions to myself when it comes to your family?" Katherine questions with an arched eyebrow.

I raise my hands in defeat. "Alright, baby, I got you."

"I'll take care of my family's issues on my own. All you've got to do is look pretty."

"I thought that was your job," I say, leaning forward to kiss her softly. I slide my thumb across her lips, my voice lowering. "I just realized I didn't officially ask."

"Ask what?" she asks, her voice soft and breathy.

"You to be mine."

She smiles. "You don't need to. I'm already yours."

I stare at her for a long moment, at her flawless skin and the waves of hair spread out like she was posed for a painting. She's only wearing my shirt, but it's long enough to be decent. Sometimes it's so hard to look at her and other times it's hard to look away. She's so damn perfect.

Katherine presses her lips between her teeth, her breaths growing slower the longer I look at her. My gaze drifts down to her nipples, visible through the material of the shirt. Katherine shifts closer until I can feel the heat of her pussy searing my cock through her panties. She runs her hand down my chest, the simple touch burning like a line of fire. Her hand trails down my abs before stopping at my shorts, where she traces the waistband with a finger.

"Topher, I want…" Her hazy gaze lifts to mine.

The lust in her stare is intoxicating, drumming hot and heavy inside of me. Her hand slips beneath my shorts and over the length of my dick. I hiss through my teeth. Katherine wraps her fingers around my cock before slowly stroking it from base to the head. The motion is enough to make me lose all self-control.

I flip us until she's under me on the couch, her body molded perfectly against mine. It doesn't take long for us to get out of our clothes. Katherine moans loudly when I push two fingers inside of her. She clenches down on me so tightly,

I groan and pull my fingers free, choosing to replace them with my cock instead. I rub the head against her pussy, the heat of it almost burning. A tremble coasts through her. I lean down to kiss the top of her head.

"I really don't deserve you," I mutter.

"I don't deserve you either," she agrees. "Probably why we're so perfect for each other."

We both gasp as I ease into her slowly, sliding into her as deep as I can go. "Ah!" She screams as I pound my cock inside of her. My eyes flutter closed. Fuck, I'll never get tired of being inside this woman. The feeling of her pussy gripping my dick and squeezing it like a vise will never get old. Every cell in me aches for more.

"Please, its too much," she says causing me to slow down a little. "Want me to stop?"

She grabs my hand and intertwine our fingers before pushing her ass towards me.

"No. Faster," Katherine whispers and my slow pace explodes into dust.

I fuck her as hard as I can smashing into every wall inside of her, leaning down to kiss her lip in order to lessen the heady rush to my head. Pressure tightens at the base of my spine. Katherine's nails dig into my arm, the pain adding to the intense pleasure unfolding inside of me. She's panting as I fuck her into a haze, her head resting against my arm.

I skim my lips against her ear, my voice rough. "Come for me, princess."

She does so with a loud moan, her head lolling on my shoulder when I roll her nipple between my fingers. She shudders and clenches around me tightly, the heat sliding down to my back. My breathing ragged, I thumb her cheek softly and run my hand up my arm. My pace grows steady, less rough as I push into her with long, slow thrusts. I grab her hands, holding them above her head and grinding against her clit until she shatters again beneath me. Then I press my face into her neck as I come with a hoarse groan.

When I feel my breathing start to even out, I flip us so she's lying atop me. Katherine brushes some of my hair from my forehead, the look in her eyes somehow reverent.

"We didn't use a condom, Toph," she states.

I shut my eyes for a second. "Shit, babe. I'm sorry."

"It's fine. Let's just try to be more responsible, okay?"

I nod. "You're on the pill right?"

"Yeah."

Something flickers in her eyes at that question, though it's too fast for me to discern it. She kisses me and her lips are so soft, I part them with my own, slipping my tongue inside. The kiss goes straight to my chest, an arrow piercing my heart.

KATHERINE DECIDES to end our self-imposed quarantine two days later. She forces me to go to the auto repair shop, claiming I shouldn't neglect my duties as the boss. I know she's right, but my heart feels a little heavy as I drop her off in front of Jameson's building.

"Go," she says on a laugh. "I'll see you later."

"You could come to work with me?" I suggest, but she shakes her head.

"No. I would only distract you. Plus, I don't work there anymore—and with good reason. I'm already worried enough that someone will see us together and it'll get back to my dad."

I know she doesn't mean anything by it, but I feel a flash of irritation. She wouldn't let me take her out anywhere yesterday because we couldn't be seen in public together. I get it; the last time we went out, we were photographed and placed in a magazine. But I also want to be able to take my girl on dates to restaurants and kiss her in broad daylight without feeling like a fucking criminal.

"I'll tell him eventually," Katherine says softly, like she can read my thoughts. "But your friend Stacey's still missing. And I don't want us to make any waves while they're searching for her."

"Yeah, you're right," I mutter, feeling like a shitty person.

She's the one that'll be put in an impossible situation. I keep holding onto hope that her dad won't overreact, but I've met her father. He's not someone to be trifled with. Katherine kisses me once before stepping out of the car. I wait until she's inside the building before driving to the repair shop.

Ellis and Cara are already there. So is Rachel. She's only seventeen and working here part-time. Which is why I was pretty amused when Katherine got jealous I had hired her replacement.

"Would you look at that. The boss has arrived," Cara says, walking forward and giving me a mock bow.

"I missed you too, Car," I say dryly, looking around the shop. "How's it going?"

"Oh, you know, the usual. Your hardworking employees slaving away while you go on a random vacation. Who's the chick?"

I arch an eyebrow. "What are you talking about?"

"When guys just drop off the grid like you did, it usually means they're getting pussy. Who is it?"

I make a face at her. "Cara, please. There are minors in here."

Rachel laughs, clearly amused by what's playing out in front of her. "That's okay. I've heard worse."

"Yeah, she's heard worse. Now tell me who it is," Cara says insistently.

I sigh. "There's no girl. And even if there was, it's none of your business, Cara."

Her green eyes gleam. "You're lying. If you're going to such lengths to hide it, then it probably means this relationship is serious. Which is crazy because I've known you for years and you've never been in a serious relationship."

I give her a droll look. "Can you do me a solid and find someone with at least half the skills that you have, train them for a few weeks then quit? Cause I can use a less annoying person around me at work," I joke.

She offers me a mischievous smile. "Please. This place wouldn't last a day without me. But back to my question. I'd just like to know if there was anyone making you happy."

That's kind of sweet. I'll tell her about myself and Katherine eventually. But she's right, until we're sure about her family's reaction, it would be better to keep our relationship a secret from everyone else.

KATHERINE and I are lying in bed facing each other that night and she's trailing her hand down my bare chest when her eyes narrow.

"I just realized something," she starts.

"Oh yeah," I murmur tiredly.

"Why don't you have more tattoos? It seems weird, doesn't fit with your whole persona."

I grin. "And what persona is that?"

"I don't know. I just think you're exactly the kind of guy who goes out and gets a tattoo as soon as he turns sixteen and every month after. But you just have a couple which I think I saw on your brother as well, so I assume that's like a family thing? But that's it. Why?"

I twirl a strand of her hair in my hand distractedly. "Do you want me to get a tattoo?"

"No, I just want to know. Literally everyone else in your circle is loaded with tatts. Just wondering why not you."

"No reason," I mutter.

"Topher."

"What?" I ask on a laugh, looking away from her eyes.

She hits my chest. "Tell me the truth."

"Geez, woman. Let's keep the physical violence to a minimum."

"Don't tell me you're—" She lets out a soft gasp. "Are you afraid of needles?"

My eyes widen and I splutter, "Wh-hat? That's ridiculous, princess."

She laughs. "Oh, I am so right!"

"I'm not scared of needles, Katie."

Before I can blink, she's rolling across the bed and sitting astride me. Her hand goes down to my throat, her eyes fierce. "Tell the truth, Toph," she sings.

I cough out a laugh. "Is this really necessary?"

"Yep."

"Alright, fine. I'm not a fan of sharp things piercing my skin. Happy?"

"Very." She grins, sliding off me. "I already knew. I just wanted to hear you say it."

"How did you know?" I frown.

"Dany and I have been texting. She's the best." She laughs, while I groan softly. "Oh, and she gave me your mom's number, but I haven't texted her. I wasn't sure if you wanted her to know about us yet," she says, biting the corner of her lips.

I kiss her forehead, "Of course I want you to meet my mom. She's just intense. I'm trying to keep you to myself for a little while longer."

She giggles when I bite her ear softly, "Alright. I was actually worried. It felt like you were keeping me away from her or something."

"Please, I've told her all about you. She has probably heard more about you than anyone else and she wants so badly to meet you. I just want us to take things slow. Enjoy each other's company first before involving my crazy family."

Although it might be a little too late for that, considering Daniella.

Katherine's expression brightens. "Speaking of enjoying each other's company…"

She's practically beaming as she gets up and walks over to where her bag is in the corner of the room. I sit up, taking the time to enjoy the view of her delectable ass before she settles down beside me. There's an envelope in her hand, and inside it are two tickets to the Grand Prix.

"I figured you'd like Formula One, and I love it, too. There's a race in Miami this weekend. I figured we could fly out. It's fine if you don't want to, though." She looks so unsure, I roll my eyes.

"Are you kidding? You're literally…" I actually have no words.

I kiss her hard, trying to convey just how much she has come to mean to me and how grateful I am to have her. I stare at her for a long moment after that, her beautiful blue eyes, the smile on her face.

I've never been in love. But a part of me realizes that what I feel for Katherine might be exactly that.

CHAPTER 23

Katherine

With a shaky breath, I pull into the parking lot. I just recently got my car back from Topher's repair shop. It's good as new—he even got it repainted and added some custom seats I know must have cost a fortune. He made a lot more upgrades, and I've been worrying myself sick thinking about how I'm going to pay him back. That's the furthest thing from my mind as I step out of the car, though.

A bell dings above my head as I enter the drugstore, and my hands tremble as I find the aisle containing pregnancy tests. My period is late.

As soon as I realized it this morning, my heart climbed into my throat. I'm grateful I had spent the night at Jameson's place instead of Topher's. If Topher had seen the expression on my face, he would have known immediately that something was wrong. But it seems I'm out of luck because as soon as my hand connects with a pregnancy test, my phone starts to ring. A soft sigh escapes me.

I consider ignoring the call but if I don't pick up, he'll just get worried.

"Hey, babe," I greet.

"Hey. Where are you?" His voice sounds far-off and hollow, like he's lying upside down.

"I came to get something at the store. You?"

"At home. Waiting for you."

I laugh softly. "Anyone ever tell you that you've got attachment issues?"

"Can't help it, baby. It runs in the family. What store are you at? You need me to come get you?"

"No, it's fine. I have my car back, remember? I'll see you soon."

He grows quiet for a couple of seconds. "Katherine... tell me what's wrong."

Fuck.

"Nothing's wrong. What makes you think there's anything wrong?"

"Because you sound like you're hiding something. There was a slight hitch in your voice, and you only get that when you're lying."

I roll my eyes and lean against a wall in the store. I hate that he knows me so well.

"Where are you?" he says insistently.

"Topher," I start, then falter. If I really am pregnant, it would be life-changing for the both of us. I'm not sure how he would take it.

"You can tell me anything, princess."

I take a deep breath. We officially started dating two weeks ago. While it's not the ideal amount of time to even be discussing a pregnancy, if there's any possibility of it, he deserves to know.

"I came to buy a pregnancy test."

Topher doesn't say anything for several seconds. I have to

pull the phone from my ear to confirm he hasn't hung up. When he speaks, his voice is quieter.

"I thought you said you were on birth control."

"I was," I tell him. "I got on the pill the day after we had sex that first time. We didn't use a condom then."

"Yeah, we didn't."

I'm starting to feel a little uneasy. "Talk to me, Toph. Are you mad?"

"What? No!" he states. "Why would I be mad? Come on, baby."

"But I don't know how you're feeling right now. Screw this, I should have told you in person." My heart starts to race. I think I might be panicking.

"Katie, breathe," he says, his voice warm and comforting in my ear. "It's just a lot to think about. A baby. Damn. I wonder if she'd have your eyes," he muses.

I let out a huge breath of relief at that and smile. "She?"

"Yeah. I want a girl. Daniel needs a little cousin to play with, anyway."

Tears well up in my eyes because he's taking this so perfectly. "So you wouldn't mind? If I was really pregnant?"

"No I don't mind. It is what it is at this point princess. But our kid's grandfather will probably take me out."

I love him.

The words are on the tip of my tongue. But I can't say them to him over the phone.

"I'm coming over now," I tell him. "I can take the test with you and we can wait for the results together."

"Alright," Topher rumbles. "Drive safe, baby."

He hangs up and I smile to myself like an idiot. A few minutes ago, I was terrified out of my mind. One conversation with Topher and every doubt I've ever had is gone. He makes me feel like I can do anything, as long as he's right beside me.

I buy the pregnancy test and walk out of the store much happier than I came in. But the smile on my face vanishes when my dad's name flashes across the screen of my phone.

Shit.

"Hi, Dad," I greet, picking up.

I lean against my car, hoping the conversation will be brief.

"Katherine," he says. "How are you, honey?"

"I'm good."

"Hmm. I haven't seen you in a bit. Still staying at Jameson's place?"

"Yes," I answer, my voice tight. I still haven't forgiven him for cutting off my credit cards.

I'm just glad my best friend is rich. Initially, I felt bad about spending Jamie's money. But he has lots of it and he doesn't seem to care. Plus, I've spent almost twenty-three years taking care of him. I'll take this as my compensation.

"Really, Katherine?" my dad asks, his voice low and icy.

"Yep," I say.

"Alright. It's a good thing you've had Jamie to take care of you all this while."

More like the other way around. "Yes, Daddy."

"Do you plan on staying there long-term or are you coming back home. I'll return all your credit cards. Your punishment's over."

My eyebrows go up. My dad never backs down. Ever. I'm immediately suspicious.

"Why?"

"Because I realized I've been pushing my daughter away. And I don't want to do that anymore."

"Okay. Thanks, Dad. I really appreciate it. And for what

it's worth, I've been looking into some serious job opportunities."

It turns out I may be a mom soon so now might be time to get my life back on track.

"You can do that after you get back from Paris," he states.

I pause. "What?"

"Paris, honey. I'm sure you're aware your sister and mother left the country a few days ago."

"Yes."

"Well, I was thinking it's probably a good idea if we both go and join them. Make it a family vacation."

"Why do you suddenly want to go on vacation?" I question curiously.

"I just think it'll be good for us. We'd be out of the country and safe."

"Why aren't we safe in the country?" I ask on a laugh.

He doesn't say a word for several moments, and when he does, it's a muttered, "Of course we're safe."

"Alright. Then I'm not going."

"Katherine," he says, letting out a sigh.

"I'm staying here, Daddy."

I might be imagining it, but this conversation seems very passive aggressive. Then my dad speaks again and his tone is all aggression.

"Why? Because you'd rather stay in New York with Christopher D'Angelo?"

My jaw tightens. "I don't know what you're talking about."

"Don't lie to me, Katherine! I know you've been seeing him. I've had someone on your tail for about a week now. I know you've spent most of your nights at his house."

"That's—you had no right to do that!"

"I had every right. I'm your father. And this has gone on long enough."

I take a deep breath and force myself to calm down. "I don't know what you think you know, Daddy. But the least you can do is let me explain myself."

"Really? And what explanation could you possibly have for cavorting with the son of a criminal? A man who belongs to an entire family of them. Do you even realize how this looks?"

"Dad, forget about how it looks for a second and think about how I feel," I say desperately.

He falls silent for a beat, then he lets out a short laugh. "Please don't tell me you were foolish enough or deluded enough to fall in love with him."

His words sting. My grip on the phone tightens. "I did fall in love with him," I say confidently. "Because he's amazing. And kind and caring. He sees me for me."

My dad barks out another laugh. "You really are deluded."

"No. I'm thinking clearly, Dad."

His voice grows angrier. "Listen to me, Katherine. I've already booked our plane tickets. You will show up to this house tomorrow morning after ending things with that boy— otherwise, you are no longer my daughter."

And there it is. The ultimatum I've been waiting for. I was expecting it, and yet somehow his words still hurt.

"Then maybe I'm not your daughter anymore," I say tearfully.

Before he can speak again, I hang up the phone. I'll probably regret that in a few minutes. Like it or not, I'm going to show up tomorrow. And I'll sit him down and try my hardest to make him see things from my perspective. He probably won't, but at least I'll know I tried.

One thing I know for sure is that I'm not leaving Topher. Not now, not ever.

I start to drive to his house on autopilot. I'm about ten minutes from the drugstore when my car starts acting up. I manage to drive it to the side of the road before it stutters to a stop. I stare for several minutes, dumbfounded.

Why the fuck is this happening to me?

Groaning softly, I step outside and pop the hood. I just got it back yesterday; it should be good as new. After checking to see if it's an issue I can fix, I call Topher. He picks up on the first ring and I quickly tell him what's wrong.

"I'm not sure what happened. It was fine when I drove it earlier and now there's smoke everywhere."

"What?" he says, confused. "That doesn't make any sense. I made sure everything was in perfect shape."

I shrug, "It's okay. Accidents happen. Can you come pick me up?"

"I'm on my way, princess."

He hangs up and I shiver, rubbing my arms. The road's pretty much deserted. It almost reminds me of that first night Topher and I met. We were such different people back then. Especially him, he's changed so much.

A car starts driving toward me from the other direction, and I pray silently that whoever's in it won't stop. Unfortunately, the car does stop, a few feet away from me. A man steps out.

He's wearing a baseball hat and a face mask below his eyes. I immediately get a bad feeling. I rush to my car door, to lock myself inside or at least grab the pepper spray I keep in my purse. He starts to run toward me. I turn my back for one second, which is when something hard hits my head, and I go down immediately. The last thing I see before I pass out are green eyes filled with malice.

WHEN I WAKE UP, I'm inside a dark room. I sit up with a gasp and rub the back of my head, where a lump has formed. My throat goes dry because this situation feels all too familiar. But I can't let myself panic yet. Very slowly, I get to my feet. A movement in a corner causes me to startle. I whirl around and see someone seated in the corner. A girl, with olive skin and dark hair.

"Who are you?" I ask, fighting to fight down the terror clawing up my throat.

She whimpers softly. Her brown eyes are hollow. She looks thin and starved. I move toward her but she inches away. She's obviously scared out of her mind. I raise both hands up.

"Hey, I'm not going to hurt you. I promise. My name's Katherine. What's yours?"

Her voice is hoarse when she speaks. "Stacey," she replies. "My name is Stacey."

I let out a soft gasp. "Stacey?" There's no way. "Do you know the D'Angelos?"

She nods vigorously as tears pool in their eyes. "I do. I've spent the past month hoping someone would come to save me. Christian," she gasps. "Why hasn't Christian come for me yet?"

My vision feels a little blurry. I'm actively trying not to think about how small this room is. Or the darkness surrounding me. There's a small lightbulb on the wall that keeps flickering on and off, but apart from that, the room is pretty sparse.

"He's been trying. Stacey, do you know where we are? Who has us?"

She opens her mouth to reply but then there's the sound of

a door being unlocked. Stacey inches closer to the wall, cowering in horror. Someone climbs down the stairs. My heart starts to race and then it stutters to a stop when I'm face to face with a face I've only seen in my worst nightmares.

"Hello, Katherine."

Charles Leeman grins as he stares at me with a hungry expression. He's larger than he was six years ago, more menacing, with tattoos trailing up his arms and a large scar on the side of his face. I don't move, I don't even breathe. I just stand there, disbelieving.

This is a dream. This has to be a dream. I repeat the words in my head over and over again like a chant.

Then he advances on me. Before I can blink, I'm on the floor. My cheeks sting where he hit me. He leans down and sneers, "That was for calling the cops on me the last time, bitch."

"How—"

"How am I standing here free? I got out on parole, sweetheart. Been a model prisoner the last six years. Your daddy didn't tell you? I came here for you and your sister. As soon as I got free. I wanted you both. But Tessa's not in New York anymore, is she?"

I'm suddenly very glad Tessa already left with Mom. If not, I don't doubt she'd have been in here with me. My sister suffered so much the last time, she doesn't deserve to be near him ever again. But he's been watching us, and the knowledge causes my skin to crawl. My fists tighten as I stare him down, drawing on all the willpower I've got. My stomach churns—from fear, from nausea, I'm not sure.

"How did you find me?" I ask.

"I've been watching you. I followed you when you left your friend's house this morning. Luckily for me, you were all alone. I messed with your car when you went into that drugstore. Then I waited for you to drive past me."

He's planned it all meticulously. Down to every last detail. I start to feel faint. Leeman gets back to his feet and glances at Stacey with a self-satisfied smirk.

"Get comfortable, Katherine. Because you're never getting out of here."

I can't breathe. I think I'm hyperventilating. Or dying. Leeman offers a cruel smirk as he stares down at me. It isn't until he walks out and closes the basement door that I allow the darkness to swallow me.

CHAPTER 24

Topher

Charles Bukowski once said, "Find what you love and let it kill you."It's a quote I've always liked, and it's been burned into my brain for years. It's never made more sense to me than it does in this moment. It honestly feels like I might die right now. Because Katherine's gone. And I have no idea where she is.

I called my brothers first and then I called the cops ten minutes ago. It's been twenty minutes since I got here to pick up my girl, thinking she'd be waiting for me. But she was gone. Her phone was on the ground, her purse was on the chair but she was nowhere to be found.

Something icy had slid up my veins. I'd yelled her name for two minutes and then I called for help. Then I made a call to a place I could never have imagined before today, the FBI office and asked for James Malone.

My brothers get here first. Then the cops and, finally, Katherine's father arrive. He beelines for me and I barely have any time to prepare before he throws a punch at my jaw. I'm not sure I could have dodged it even if I wanted to. I'm numb. Carlo has to physically restrain him.

"You motherfucker!" James Malone yells. "This is all your fault. You and your fucking family. I knew this would happen."

"Calm the hell down," Christian orders sharply, staring down at the older man. "We had nothing to do with this."

One of the cops walks over, asking for my statement. I tell them everything.

"She told me she'd wait for me here. I was coming to pick her up," I say.

The officer in front of me nods. "And she didn't give you any inclination that she would get a ride elsewhere?"

My eyes narrow into a glare. "What are you insinuating? That she left on her own? Without her phone or her purse?"

"I'm trying not to rule out possible explanations, sir," the officer says. He glances nervously at my brother beside me. I guess Christian's reputation precedes him. "In cases like this, the victim probably disappeared on her own."

"That's fucking bullshit," I state.

"Sir—"

"Enough!" Malone yells. He fixes his tie before shoving Carlo away and stepping forward. He looks at the officer. "This is a federal investigation now."

"Doesn't that seem a little rash?" Christian drawls.

"Katherine was kidnapped."

Blood rushes to my head at that. I keep imagining her somewhere, scared out of her mind.

"That seems obvious enough," Christian states, staring at him. "But we can't rule out that it could be a hostage situation that can be easily resolved." His eyes flick to me. "Someone might have taken her due to her affiliations with my family."

"Oh, I have no doubt that your family of criminals has no shortage of enemies that would want to harm my daughter for associating with you," he says, his blue eyes icy and hard. "But unfortunately, I know exactly who has my daughter."

"Who?" I ask through gritted teeth.

Malone looks away. Fear flickers in his expression. "Charles Leeman was released from jail two months ago."

It takes me a minute to place the name. When I do, I'm walking forward and grabbing the man at the collar of his shirt.

"Please tell me you're fucking joking."

He's taller than me. His expression remains cool as he stares down at me.

"I wish I was. I only just found out a week ago. I was hoping to get her out of the country until we could confirm his whereabouts," he says.

I let him go and start to pace. "If that bastard has her..." I can't even finish the sentence.

"Leeman has some odd revenge fantasy against me. He wants to hurt me."

"I'll hurt you for him if he gives me Katherine back," I mutter.

Beside me, Christian's lips curl into a smile. Malone glares. "Unfortunately, that's not an option. I have all the resources of the FBI at my disposal. I'll find my daughter."

Christian places his hand on my shoulder. He gives me a reassuring look. "We'll find her, *fratello*."

THE COMBINED efforts of both my family and the FBI yield a lot of answers to a lot of questions. Surprisingly, James Malone seems inclined to provide us with any information we need. As Christian pointed out, he isn't stupid. He understands that we have a lot more manpower to provide. And more eyes and ears in every corner of New York.

In a matter of hours, I know everything there is to know about the man who has Katherine. Charles Leeman is a forty-five-year-old man who spent the last six years in a penitentiary in New Jersey. He was released on parole two months ago thanks to a spotless record during his time served. He was sent home with an ankle monitor to ensure he didn't violate the terms of his release. He wasn't supposed to leave his town of residence and yet he somehow found his way to New York two months ago.

The first thing we work on is finding out how he worked his way around the ankle monitor. It's increasingly clear that he's not working alone. Someone's been helping him. Someone good with computers, someone who was able to reroute the information on the ankle monitor and make it so that it seemed like Leeman hadn't taken it off at all.

It takes us two days to find out who. A friend of Leeman's who had apparently grown up with him. Malone made some calls to Jersey, sending people to detain him. He left a few hours ago to interrogate the guy while we've stayed behind to keep searching.

"I have a gut feeling," Christian says, walking into his office. He's been going back and forth between the FBI office, home, and here. He's the one running this operation and keeping it together.

I haven't left this room in two days. I can barely sleep or eat. Every time I close my eyes, I see Katherine's eyes. Or I hear her calling for me. It's driving me crazy.

"What gut feeling?" Carlo questions, getting to his feet.

"Stacey disappeared around the same time Leeman showed up in the city," he murmurs.

My eyes widen as I realize what he's hinting at. "You don't think he has her, do you?"

A part of me had been holding on to hope that Stacey chose to disappear on her own.

"It's possible," Christian says, taking a seat at his desk. He grabs his laptop, turning it on. "There aren't any CCTV cameras where she was taken but..." He trails off, turning his attention to his laptop.

His hands move over the keys furiously and I watch as he hacks into several security cameras around the city. We followed Stacey and Leeman to the same shopping center. He must have taken her near the back where there are no cameras and then we see a car drive off but one different from the one he drove there in.

"The bastard has Stacey," Carlo says, his jaw clenched.

It doesn't make any sense, though. Why would he kidnap Stacey? She doesn't know Katherine or the Malones.

"This is good," Christian says, distracting me from my thoughts. "We can narrow it down now. I just need to cross-examine the places where their locations overlap and try to find the vehicle he used to abduct Katherine yesterday. Get Malone on the phone. I can't do this on my own."

Soon enough, we've got the best computer experts on the case. Christian tells me it might take a few hours until they're able to get the exact location. All we can do is wait.

"Tomorrow, Topher," Carlo says, placing a hand on my shoulder. "We'll know where they are by tomorrow."

CHAPTER 25

Katherine

I t's been two days. Leeman spent the first day coming in here every two hours. He didn't say anything, he simply stared at both of us with a self-satisfied smirk on his face. When he moved to touch me, I put up a fight, scratching his face till it bled. He stayed away after that.

Yesterday, he told me the story of how he abducted Stacey. He was so pleased with himself.

"I thought she was Tessa," he said laughing. "She was on the phone with your daddy if you can believe that. Talking about the D'Angelo's and I just couldn't believe it. It was like a gift from the man upstairs. I knew I had to act fast and by the time I realized it wasn't your sister, it was too late. Either way, I figured she'd be useful in one way or another," he said leaning down to touch her bare arms causing her to flinch.

I hate that he kidnapped Stacey but I am so grateful it wasn't Tessa. Leeman also informed us that we'd be moved soon. He was going to take us somewhere else. To his hometown. He also said he might have to kill one of us but he wouldn't tell us who. According to him, he's grown pretty attached to Stacey in the month since he's had her.

Stacey didn't talk much until after Leeman told us that he'd kill one of us. Once he left, I couldn't help but ask her how she knew my father.

She said he reached out to her during his investigation into the D'Angelo family hoping she would be helpful to bring the down.

"Are you an informant for the FBI? Were you going to help take them down?" I asked shocked knowing how much the family cared for her. "No. Never. I've told your dad repeatedly that I wouldn't. I couldn't. But he's persistent. Christian is the reason I grew up an orphan and I'll never really forgive them for killing my father. But, he's human and he did what he thought was right. Also, their family has tried their best to look after me and I appreciate that. Some things are just unforgivable you know. But I would never work against them. The truth is my dad was a part of the dark world, so he was no saint. I just didn't want to lose him," she said a tear rolling down her cheek.

Then she started to ask me questions. She wanted to know how I knew the D'Angelos, so I told her about Topher. She told me about law school and her friends and the boyfriend she had to break up with because she thought he was a distraction.

We're both trying to find some solace in each other while we wait for the people we love to come save us.

"I might be pregnant," I confess to Stacey on the third day.

She arches an eyebrow. "You got knocked up by a D'Angelo? Shit, dude."

I almost laugh. "Yeah, yeah, I did. It's not so bad, though."

"Hmm. Who do you think deserves to live more?" Stacey wonders aloud. "You're pregnant, sure. But I just graduated. I spent the last six years of my life studying my ass off. You think that trumps pregnancy?" she asks laughing.

"That's a pretty cynical question, Stacey."

She snorts. "I'm a cynical person. I've had to be. I lost my papa when I was thirteen. The closest thing I have to a family is my aunt. And, oddly enough, the people responsible for my dad's death."

"I'm sorry, Stacey," I say quietly.

She shakes her head. "It wasn't so bad. Like I said, the D'Angelos took care of me. Carman was a bastard but he was a bastard that cared for his own. He loved those three boys so much; I saw it all first-hand. All it did was make me miss my dad, though. He's the one that wanted me to become a lawyer. He said he'd always need legal representation in his course of work and he wasn't ready to pay all those damn lawyer fees."

She laughs softly at the memory.

"You think he made it to heaven?"

Her brown eyes meet mine. I can tell she's starting to unravel. She's been down here for more than a month. It's enough to drive a person crazy.

"I couldn't tell you, Stacey."

"That's alright. He probably didn't. He wasn't a good man. I'm sure he met Daddy D'Angelo in hell."

It unsettles me to hear her talking about Topher's dad like that. Then again, she's probably right.

"You're lucky you got the good one," Stacey says like she can read my thoughts. "Topher's wild and reckless, but he's got a pretty good heart at his core."

That makes me smile. "He's changed a lot in the past few months. He's less wild and reckless."

"Good for him, then."

If I close my eyes, I can almost pretend I'm not in a dark basement. I'm having a conversation with a new friend.

We're bonding, and everything's okay. Then there's the sound of footsteps and my fantasy shatters.

Nothing's okay. I'm terrified it never will be.

"Who do you think he's going to kill?" Stacey asks.

"Probably me," I reply quietly. "He's waited six years to kill me. He's not going to hesitate."

Stacey gives me a sharp look. "You're not dying. You've got a little baby growing in there."

I smile. "And you just finished law school. You've got a whole career as a badass lawyer."

"Exactly."

Light floods the room and I squint as Leeman climbs down the ladder. He doesn't close the hatch. He's dressed in black, a gun holster at his side. My heart pounds and blood roars in my ears.

Oh, God, please, please, please. If I'm really pregnant, don't let my baby get hurt.

"The FBI's breathing down my neck," he mutters. "They're going to storm in here soon. I can feel it."

I force myself not to show any signs of hope. Leeman glares at me.

"This is all your dad's fault, you know. And her family, as well," he says, pointing at Stacey. "I wouldn't have taken her if I knew her family was connected to the underworld. How the hell does that even happen huh? How unlucky can I be? Shit!"

We don't say a word as he paces in front of us, muttering to himself. I don't think he's completely sane. Which is bewildering to me because how on earth was he able to act normal enough in jail to be let out on parole so early?

"I can't get out of the state. There's police checkpoints everywhere. Men from her family are going all around the city, looking everywhere. Some of them are in the next street over. They could find this place at any moment." He stops pacing and glares. "This is all your fucking fault!"

He grabs his gun and points. My entire body tenses.

"Charles, wait," I say. "You don't want to shoot us."

He shakes his head. "No, no, I think I do. Maybe I'll shoot you both and then I'll kill myself. There's some justice in that, isn't there?"

My mind whirs as I think of a way to stall him. "No, think about your brother. Your brother's still in jail, isn't he? Are you going to kill yourself and lose the chance to ever see him again?"

Stacey speaks up, playing along. "If you turn yourself in, I'm sure you could negotiate some terms with the DA's office. Maybe they'll even let you stay in the same prison as your brother. You could be reunited."

That's actually a pretty solid deal. I don't know if Stacey's lying or if it's actually possible, but Leeman hesitates, seemingly intrigued by the idea. While he thinks it over, Stacey and I slowly get to our feet.

"You don't have to kill us, Charles," I say softly.

His eyes flick to mine and my blood chills at the look in them.

"I'm not going to let you go free, little girl. Especially not you." His hands are steady as he points the gun at my head. "This is for my brother."

I wish I had just told Topher I loved him.

My eyes fly shut as a pop sounds. "No!" Stacey screams.

She pushes me out of the way and the bullet hits her shoulder instead. I gasp, my hand immediately closing over the bullet hole on her arm. The two of us go down, me crouching over her, trying to do what I can to help. Tears fill my vision.

"Why did you do that?" I ask.

"You're carrying a D'Angelo baby," she says weakly. "I owe that family a debt. I guess this is my way of repaying it."

"Oh god, oh god," I say, breathing heavily. More and more blood is seeping out of the wound and I don't know how to stop it.

Then there's a sharp tug on my hair as I'm pulled to my feet. I struggle against Leeman's grip.

"Please, please, let me help her."

Stacey's eyes are shut and she's turning pale. She's still losing blood.

"Shut up! If she dies, she dies. You're next."

Someone jumps down the hatch, surprising Leeman. He whirls us around and my heart practically stops. Topher's here. He falters when he sees me, his eyes dropping to the blood on my hands. Then he pulls a gun out in a fluid motion, aiming it at Leeman.

"Who the hell are you?" Leeman snarls.

"Someone who's about to murder you," Topher states, his eyes hard.

Leeman's grip on me tightens and he presses the barrel of his gun against my head.

"Let her go," Topher says, ice in his voice. His hands tighten around the gun he's holding.

"I don't think so."

The gun presses harder onto the side of my head. I'm immobilized by fear. The only thing that feels real are Topher's eyes, which are growing more and more terrified with each passing moment. I try to communicate to Topher how much I love him. Footsteps sound in the distance; I can hear people running. We're out of time. Leeman's going to shoot.

He leans down to whisper in my ear, "Good bye, little Malone."

Topher's gun goes off at that exact moment. Leeman drops to the ground behind me. I gasp, whirling around to see blood seeping from a bullet wound on his chest. My legs wobble and I would have crashed to the ground, but Topher's here—holding me, hugging me.

"You're okay, Katherine. You're okay," he whispers, kissing the side of my forehead.

Several men start to climb down the ladder. I catch sight of Topher's eldest brother running to check on Stacey. Topher and I are on the ground, but I don't know how we got there.

"You shot him," I say softly.

Topher's brown eyes darken. "He didn't give me a choice."

CHAPTER 26

Topher

For some reason, I thought it would be more painful, taking a life. Instead, all I feel is cold and empty. Numb at the thought. And something else—immense relief.

Katherine's in my arms and she's safe. She passes out on the way to the hospital. Mental exhaustion and severe dehydration, according to the paramedics. Stacey's rushed into emergency surgery as soon as we arrive. Katherine kept on mumbling over and over that Stacey saved her.

I spent the next few hours sitting outside Katherine's hospital room. They gave her something to sleep and have been monitoring her. She hasn't woken up yet, and neither has Stacey. I feel helpless again, like I can't control anything.

Carlo's beside me, offering strength and quiet reassurance. I'm not sure where Christian is, but my best guess is that he's taking care of this entire fucked-up situation. My brothers are a gift, the best gift I could have ever asked for. I'm not sure what I would have done in this situation without them.

My hands haven't stopped shaking since we arrived at the hospital. Not since they took Katherine away.

"Toph," Carlo says, drawing my attention to someone walking over.

I stand to my feet and meet James Malone's eyes. I guess he's back from Jersey.

"How is she?" he questions gruffly.

"We're about to find out," I tell him as the doctor exits her hospital room.

The man offers us a small smile. "The patient's not in any danger. She has a few bruises, but otherwise she's in perfect condition. Both her and the baby."

Baby?

I had been so focused on getting her back, it had slipped my mind that Katherine mentioned that she might be pregnant. My heart aches when I realize I almost lost two people instead of one. If I had gotten to that cellar a little later... If I hadn't been quick enough. I start to feel a little lightheaded.

James Malone's furious blue eyes find mine. But he doesn't approach me or say anything about me impregnating his daughter.

"Can I see her, Doctor?" Malone asks, a slight tremble in his voice.

The doctor nods. "Let's just try not to upset her too much. She's still in a pretty delicate condition. A nurse will direct you to the room."

He walks away and a nurse arrives to inform us that Katherine would like to see her father. It stings a little that she didn't ask for me first, but I get it. Her dad still hasn't seen her, but I rode to the hospital with her and held her hand. She can take her time.

Although there's a seed of doubt starting to grow in my mind. What if she doesn't want me anymore? What if taking a life actually did change me, and the most important person in my life can see those changes woven into me better than I can?

Christian calls to inform us that Stacey's awake, so Carlo and I head up to her room. He's already talking to her when we arrive. I take note of the relief in Christian's eyes. He looks more at ease than I've seen him in weeks.

"You look rough, Stace," I say, taking her in.

She's paper-thin and pale, but at least she's alive. We almost lost her.

"Did you hear I saved your baby?" she questions, her voice weak and quiet.

I nod. "Yeah, Katherine said we might have to make you the baby's godmother."

It's one of the things she whispered to me. In those few minutes it took before we got to the hospital.

Stacey laughs softly. "Sounds like work. I didn't do it for that."

"So why did you do it?" I question, sounding a little out of breath.

"I wasn't about to let a little D'Angelo die," she whispers.

Christian's jaw clenches. "You shouldn't have had to go through that. I'm sorry, Stace."

"I'm alright. At least I'm still alive. I'm looking at each one of your handsome faces." She smirks.

I chuckle. At least she still has her sense of humor intact.

"Where's my aunt?" she asks.

Carlo answers, "She's on her way. She'll be here in a bit."

"Okay. That bastard's really dead, right?" she asks, her eyes darting to me. "He's gone?"

I nod. "He's gone, Stace. He can't hurt you anymore."

She relaxes, letting the tension melt from her body. "Alright. Alright. I think I need to rest, guys."

We walk out, weighed down heavily by all that's happened in the past few days. It feels like my life was thrown upside down and I have no idea how to get it back on track. My brothers look at me, and I already know what's coming before they speak.

"I'm fine," I mutter at the expressions on their faces.

"The first's one's always the hardest," Carlo says, his jaw tight.

"You don't have to be fine, little brother," Christian agrees.

"Are you kidding? I've got a woman to take care of and a baby on the way. I have to be fine, Chris."

His cool brown eyes roam across my face, searching, studying.

"I guess you're right," he finally says. "If you need anything, though."

"I know. I'm just going to head over to Katherine's room."

They let me go while they wait for Stacey's aunt and our mom to arrive. Mom was probably going through it these past few days, worried sick.

When I get back to Katherine's room, her father's exiting. There's a smile on his face, but he takes one look at me and it vanishes.

"She's looking for you," he informs me. I move to walk in, but he stops me. "Thank you. For saving her."

I stare at him, then offer a single nod of acknowledgment. "I did what I had to."

He looks away. I open the door and walk into her hospital room after a quick breath of hesitation. Katherine's seated with a sad expression she quickly puts away once I step in.

"Hey," she breathes, gesturing for me to take her hand. I

move closer and do so, and the trembling stops. My demons go quiet at the sight of her. "How's Stacey?"

"She's out of danger. I just spoke to her and she seems okay," I inform her.

Katherine nods, looking relieved. We don't say anything for several minutes. My gaze roams over her hungrily, trying to memorize every inch of her. I can't count the amount of times I imagined finding her dead, or even worse.

"You almost died," I say, my voice hoarse.

Katherine's gaze is steady. "I didn't."

"But you almost died. You had a bullet to your head right in front of me. You have no idea how fucking terrified I was, princess. I thought I would lose you."

She grips my hand harder. "You didn't. I'm fine, I promise. Just pregnant," she murmurs.

"How did your dad take it?"

"He didn't," she admits. "He didn't say a word about it. He was just relieved that I'm alive, I guess. He hugged me and told me he loved me, then apologized for fighting with me so much the past few weeks."

I don't know what to say to that. Katherine continues regardless.

"Topher, listen. He asked me to go to Paris with him. Just for a little while."

Something icy slides up my veins at that.

"My mom and sister are worried sick. He didn't tell them what happened to me until this morning. They want to fly back immediately, but they still have some things to take care of over there, so Dad said we should go."

I'm really trying to be rational here but the only thing I'm hearing is that she wants to leave me. I let out a shaky breath.

"Do you have to go?"

She nods. "I promise I'll come back."

My hand tightens around hers. "Then why do I have this hollow feeling in my chest? Why does it feel like I'm losing you?"

"You would never lose me," Katherine says sharply. "First off, there's a little baby growing inside of me that belongs to us both. And also," she whispers, "I love you, Topher D'Angelo."

She lets out a soft breath as tears well up in her eyes. "You have no idea how many times I wanted to say those words in the past two days. I almost thought I'd never get to say it."

My hand brushes her cheek, slowly, reverently. "Life used to be so easy before you came around. I was coasting through it without a care in the world. Everything was so simple."

"I'm sorry I ruined that for you," Katherine says dryly.

I roll my eyes. "Calm down, let me finish. I didn't realize how empty it was. I wasn't really living. There's a difference between existing and living. You taught me how to live, princess. You made every single day worth it because I'd get to wake up and see your face. Even when we were pretending to be friends, a part of me has always known you're it for me. Always will be."

"That was a lot of words to tell me you love me," Katherine says, smiling.

I'm kissing her in the next breath, unable to hold myself back anymore. "I love you, princess. *Per sempre.*" Forever.

She shifts to let me climb onto the hospital bed beside her. I hold her for as long as I can, trying to wipe the past few days from my mind.

"What if it changed me, killing Leeman?"

"It didn't. You're still the man I love. And don't you dare think about feeling guilty. You did what you had to do. You saved us... all three of us." Her hand grazes my cheek. "I see you, Topher. All of you."

She kisses me again, harder this time. I try not to think of it as a farewell, but it's pretty hard not to when she won't be going home in my arms. I never thought I could love someone so much.

CHAPTER 27

Katherine

ONE MONTH LATER

Topher returns home and finds me leaning against the door of his condo. He stills in his steps, his eyes piercing into mine.

"Surprise," I say on a laugh.

He doesn't even hesitate. He rushes forward and pulls me into his arms. I press my face into his chest, my entire body shaking. He feels so right, so warm, so comforting, that the back of my eyes burn.

"Fuck, princess," he whispers, holding me like I'm the only precious thing in the world.

I lean away to look him in the eyes, seeing how much he cares. How vulnerable his expression is.

"I know. I missed you like hell, too."

One of his hands grips my neck possessively while the other coasts across my lips. My breath hitches. He pulls me in and kisses me deeply. I sigh into his mouth, heat washing down to my toes. My hands curl around his neck and Topher groans in satisfaction, kissing me so hard it steals every single breath away. When we finally let go, there's enough heat searing in his gaze that it causes my insides to melt.

He doesn't let go of my hand as I follow him inside. I tell him about getting a ticket to come home a few days ago because I missed him so much. Topher smiles before heading into his room. When he returns, he's holding two first-class tickets for a plane to France tomorrow.

"I guess I beat you to the punch." I grin.

He smiles, kissing my forehead once.

"Who's the second ticket for?" I question.

"My mom. She's been riding up my ass for weeks wanting to meet you. When I told her I was going, she insisted on coming along."

I smile. "I want to meet her, too. We can go tomorrow."

"Yeah, alright," Topher agrees.

He sits down on the couch, pulling me into his lap. The sight of him fills me with a heavy longing that spreads through my veins. I run my hand through his dark hair and across his face, scared that if I blink, he'll disappear.

"You need a haircut," I murmur.

"You can cut it for me," he returns, his hand tightening around my waist. "I don't think I need to tell you that I'm not letting you out of my sight for the foreseeable future, right?"

I laugh. "That seems a little dramatic."

"Tell me about Paris," he urges.

So I do. Jameson came to join us, as well—he and my sister finally got together. She finally admitted her husband had left her for his secretary but she was too embarrassed to tell us. She kept making excuses as to why he was never around but she finally came clean and now is with her true love. That was the best part about being there. Seeing the two of them happy after such a long time. My parents were pretty shocked but ultimately they let it slide, choosing to focus their energy on me.

"There was a lot of fighting," I tell Topher. "A lot of arguing. Mom actually tried to talk me into getting an abortion."

Topher stiffens at that and I quickly reassure him.

"Don't worry, I shot down her suggestion immediately. Nobody's harming our baby," I say protectively. I've spent the past month coming to terms with the fact that I'm about to become a mother. And falling in love every day with the baby growing inside of me. "Anyway, I finally appeased my dad by telling him I'd get a job at the Met."

Topher arches an eyebrow. "You don't have to work. And you certainly don't have to take a job you don't want."

"I do want it, actually," I tell him, smiling. "Working with archaeological artifacts has always been my dream. I always knew I'd end up in a museum. I guess I just wanted to be sure it was what I really wanted. And what do you mean, I don't have to work?"

"I'd take care of you," he says seriously. "I have lots and lots of money."

"That belongs to your brother," I point out. "And your family."

He grins. "I make a decent amount from the repair shop too, princess."

I roll my eyes. "Whatever. You're not making me into some sort of housewife. I'm going to work."

"Fine. You can work."

"I'm so glad I have your permission," I scoff.

Topher chuckles, pulling me closer. "God, I missed you so much."

"I missed you, too," I say softly. "Although you might change your mind soon. I've been puking my guts out every morning for the past few days. Morning sickness is awful."

"In that case, you can go sit over there," he says

pretending to throw me off him only to pull me back in and hug me.

"And I've been sleeping a lot," I point out.

I don't know why I'm listing all this out to him. The expression on his face is amused as he shakes his head.

"Shut up, Katherine," he mutters. "You're carrying our baby. None of that matters, I'll take care of you. I love you so damn much."

My heart races in my chest. Those are my favorite words to hear. "I love you, too."

He kisses me then, and the kiss is hard and heady with desire. Our movements grow frenzied, Topher hurriedly helping me out of my clothes. When he thrusts into me, I let out a soft gasp. It feels like a homecoming.

I never knew a person could qualify as a home, but Topher has proven it time and time again. Every time I sought him out over the past few months, every time I drifted towards him, it was because a part of me could recognize that he was home. Even if it took the rest of me so long to come to the same conclusion.

I found my happiness.

Topher

FOUR YEARS LATER

"Dinner's ready, everyone!" My mother's voice resonates from the bustling kitchen, her culinary talents now rivaling those of any Michelin-starred chef, all thanks to Daniel.

They say children utter the most unexpected things, and it was the moment my son told his grandmother that the painstakingly crafted cake she had spent two days making was "so gross" that my mother decided to embark on her culinary journey. With ample time during the day, she honed her craft to perfection.

One by one, we gather around the table and take our seats.

"I can't believe the friggin' D'Angelo family is at my dinner table for Thanksgiving," James chuckles.

"Tell me about it," Christian chimes in, sharing a knowing glance with me and Carlo before rolling his eyes.

Just as Katherine's dad was about to launch into his usual spiel about how he would willingly throw all of us in jail for just about anything, Christopher Jr. entered the room, brimming with childlike excitement.

"Grandpa, look what I made!" he exclaims, thrusting a meticulously crafted paper plane toward Katherine's dad.

"Whoa, you made that?" James' eyes widen with genuine astonishment. "Now there's a D'Angelo I can hang with!" He springs up from his seat, eager to play with Junior, momentarily setting aside his tough exterior.

Katherine's hand finds mine, and our wedding rings nestled perfectly atop each other.

"I'm happy for you baby brother but do you guys think he'll ever let up?" he asks.

"We're still waiting for him to bless our marriage," I quip, a hint of playful exasperation in my voice.

Stacey joined in the banter with a hearty laugh. "You guys have been married for three years!" she pointed out.

"Exactly!" I retort, raising an eyebrow.

Laughter bubbles up within us, a testament to the camaraderie we have built over the years. We watch as Katherine's dad revels in his time with Junior, his stern façade temporarily forgotten.

As our laughter subsides, a smile tugs at the corners of Katherine's dad's lips, unable to resist the infectious joy in the room.

We have come a long way from our tumultuous past, and moments like these served as poignant reminders of the power of forgiveness, love, and the unexpected twists that life can bring.

Finding joy in a love that was once… forbidden.

THE END

Did you like this book? Then you'll love … The Don, Christian D'Angelo's love story:

MARRYING THE DON OF FURY
An Arranged Marriage, Enemies to Lovers Mafia Romance

I'm getting married in a few months, and I just found out five minutes ago.

My first reaction was, 'No thanks!' But it turns out that my fiancé is the powerful don of NYC, and 'no' is not an option.

Christian D'Angelo is so gorgeous that his presence can kill, but he gladly does that with his bare hands.
I happen to be a pawn in a dangerous game to settle my family's debt.

He thought he could possess me until he realized I would not be silenced. One thing led to another, and our banter turned to lust, turned to love, and turned into a positive pregnancy test.

But I refuse to tell him because I will not be caged and thrown into his dungeon... again.

Deep down, he has a heart of gold, and I've found myself madly in love with the scariest man I've ever met.

But there is no way... I'm marrying the don of fury.

Read Marrying the Don of Fury Now!
https://www.amazon.com/dp/B0CDRNBXS8

Printed in Great Britain
by Amazon

36981500R00131